W9-AHS-328

SOME DIE ELOQUENT

"So determinedly traditional and classic . . . that almost everybody will be charmed . . . Miss Aird writes with insight and skill."
—*The New York Times Book Review*

"A tidily plotted and ends-knotted-neatly tale."
—*Publishers Weekly*

BY CATHERINE AIRD

"Aird's intelligence shines through every sentence."
—*The Washington Post*

SOME DIE ELOQUENT

BY CATHERINE AIRD

BANTAM BOOKS · TORONTO · NEW YORK · LONDON

*All of the characters in this book are fictitious,
and any resemblance to actual persons, living or dead,
is purely coincidental.*

*This low-priced Bantam Book
has been completely reset in a type face
designed for easy reading, and was printed
from new plates. It contains the complete
text of the original hard-cover edition.*
NOT ONE WORD HAS BEEN OMITTED.

SOME DIE ELOQUENT
*A Bantam Book / published by arrangement with
Doubleday & Co., Inc.*

PRINTING HISTORY
*Doubleday edition published March 1980
A Detective Book Club Alternate Selection April 1980
Bantam edition / June 1981*

ISBN 0-553-14338-7

Published in the United States and Canada

PRINTED IN THE UNITED STATES OF AMERICA

0 9 8 7 6 5 4 3 2 1

For Sylvia Cox and Norah Mallet—Scylla and Charybdis of my syntax—with love

Some die eloquent . . .
Some die wholly in half a breath
Some—give trouble for half a year.

A *Death-Bed*
by Rudyard Kipling

The chapter heads are taken from "The Canon's Yeoman's Tale" from *The Canterbury Tales* by Geoffrey Chaucer, translated into modern English by Nevill Coghill.

Chapter 1

For I imagine I have said enough
To raise the devil, be he never so rough.

It was a very long time indeed since Detective Inspector C. D. Sloan of the Criminal Investigation Department of the Berebury Division of the Calleshire County Police Force had felt such a fish out of water.

It was an unusual experience for him.

There are very few situations in daily and professional life which find your fully fledged police inspector at a real disadvantage. In the nature of things, by the time a man has reached that particular rank, working experience alone has made him ready and confident for the holding of rule, and life itself has taught him not only his own place in the world, but that such niches come in all sizes.

Actually it was his place in the world at this particular moment that was the whole trouble with Detective Inspector Sloan. Whatever his rightful position in the cosmos was on a normal Tuesday afternoon (on duty, probably, and very much for preference) he didn't really want to be where he happened to be now. Moreover, for a man whose collar had given up feeling tight in tricky situations a long time ago, who knew what to do with his hands, and who wasn't conspicuously large for a policeman, he was feeling very uncomfortable.

He had known beforehand that he would and had said as much.

It had done him no good at all.

"It's not a lot to ask, is it?" his wife, Margaret, had said to that.

1

"No."

"One afternoon."

"I could make a start on the decorating," he had offered, "instead."

The corners of his wife's mouth had twitched at the very idea.

"The back bedroom's got to be done," he had said.

"It'll get done," Margaret Sloan had replied serenely.

"Before . . ."

"Before."

He had tried another tack.

"There's a villain . . ."

"Yes?"

"I've been keeping him under observation."

"Have you?"

"All the week."

"Well?"

"He might try something on Tuesday."

"In the middle of the afternoon?"

"He doesn't like night work."

"But"—her mouth twitched again—"he does like Tuesdays?"

"You never know."

"And now," his wife had pronounced sweetly, "you never will know, will you?"

He had given in meekly enough after that at the time but now that he was here he didn't feel any better about it. Accidents and incidents, charge room and court room, cottage and castle, had found the man unperturbed, his savoir-faire unshaken: but this was different.

"Of course," said Margaret Sloan, leading the way, "if you're afraid of hospitals . . ."

Sloan wasn't afraid of hospitals. He was even familiar with this one—the Berebury District General Hospital. Well, with certain parts of it, that is. All policemen got to know specialised corners of their local hospital over the years: the Casualty Department for a start, though they called that something else now. As they'd changed the name of so many other things these days, they'd changed the name of that lately too.

Accident and Emergency Department they called it

now: not that that fooled anyone. It was still where they took you if you smashed your car up or tried to cut your throat. And where you took the small children who stuffed beads up their noses or who had swallowed Mummy's pills. Or Pills. Or detergents. Safe as houses was an expression that never misled an ambulanceman.

Variety was the essence, of course. That was why Casualty sisters stayed so long on the job. Like station sergeants, they had some of the action, all of the interest, and very little of the routine which stultified lesser mortals. They took on all comers, in fact.

And when Sister Casualty—Sloan didn't suppose for a single moment that she thought of herself by any other name—had troublemakers in her patch she would ring down to the police station. There her soul mate in office so to speak—the Berebury station sergeant—very soon had someone around to sort out the drunk and the drugged. She had her own ways of dealing with the merely belligerent.

Detective Inspector Sloan knew her department well enough. It was this part of the hospital—where he was now—that he had never been in before today.

"Other husbands come," his wife had told him by way of encouragement.

That fact had not been a great deal of consolation at the time when she had said it and was absolutely none at all now. This was because as far as he could see there was only one other husband in sight.

"There," said Mrs. Sloan triumphantly, "I said you wouldn't be the only one."

"That," muttered Sloan, "is not the point."

"Isn't one other man enough?" asked his wife, settling down on a regulation hospital chair.

"Quite enough."

"Well, then . . ."

It wasn't that only one other husband wasn't enough either: policemen weren't shy.

"It's Larky Nolson," said Sloan distantly.

Being bracketed even in the same category group of husband with Larky Nolson was no cause for gratification in a self-respecting policeman. The kindest thing you could say about Larky was that he was an ethical cripple: and they didn't have a department which dealt with that sort of deformity at the Berebury District General Hospital.

Yet.

It would come, of course. In time. In a Brave New World. Born out of Science by Experiment or realised by Accidental Observation sired by Man Leaning on a Gate. Either way it would be called progress. And they didn't have it yet.

It was about the only department missing today, conceded Sloan. There were signposts within the hospital to all sorts of places—some as unfamiliar as Cotopaxi and Popocatepetl. In fact a truly bewildering maze of corridors confronted the new arrival. They led to an even more bewildering set of departments with strange-sounding names. He for one didn't care all that much for the sound of Haematology. If they meant "blood" they should say so: and wild horses wouldn't get him near anything called Nuclear Medicine.

There was one man, though, who would have been quite at home in the main entrance. That was Inspector Harpe of Traffic Division. And he wouldn't have felt so strange because hospitals, like roads, had suddenly gone symbolic too in their direction signs. And international. Words were out; logos were in.

You didn't move to numbers either these days. Not if you weren't in the Army. Cars and people in hospitals now took direction from a series of stereotyped pictures.

They hadn't all been an unqualified success, not the road ones anyway. "Uneven Surface Ahead" and "Men Working"—an exclamation mark—brought out the ribaldry, not unconnected with Miss Mae West, down at the police station, while "Stop Children" seemed to bring out the worst in everyone. Sloan had noticed that they had their counterpart in the hospital. Here, a tooth of prehistoric dimension pointed the way to the dental department while an eye with ancient Egyptian overtones indicated the general direction of the ophthalmic clinic.

Sloan fidgeted in his chair.

They did it all by symbols these days.

Not for those who couldn't read.

But for those who couldn't understand.

Neither thinking about something else nor the fidgeting saved him from having his own eye caught by Larky Nolson.

Sloan scowled.

The last time he had seen Larky had been strictly in the line of duty. Detective Inspector Sloan's duty. It had been in the Crown Court and that meeting was the natural consequence of an earlier confrontation over a little matter of safe-breaking at a greengrocer's shop.

Larky must be out again then.

He took a quick glance at the woman sitting beside Larky and revised this. Larky must have been "outside" for some time now. Or been on parole.

Larky saw him looking his way and jerked his head towards Sloan in open recognition.

Sloan scowled again.

At least, Sloan decided, one good thing was that it was Mrs. Nolson, his wife, whom Larky was with. He hadn't gone and got some girl into trouble.

"Someone you know?" Margaret Sloan asked him cautiously.

"In a manner of speaking," said Sloan.

"Ah . . ." If you were married to a policeman you had to get used to the fact that there were some people your husband introduced to you and some he didn't.

"The greengrocer's job on the corner of Pig Lane," he said.

"I remember." Margaret Sloan nodded.

"Good," said Sloan warmly. "A good memory's important. You need it on both sides of the family."

"It was the safe, wasn't it?" said Mrs. Sloan, ignoring this.

"It was." Sloan grinned. He hadn't forgotten the detail either. Larky Nolson, small-time burglar, and Detective Inspector Sloan, policeman, had both been surprised at the amount of money in the greengrocer's safe. Mrs. Sloan, housewife, hadn't. Nor presumably had Mrs. Nolson.

"Laying up for his old age," Superintendent Leeyes

had remarked when they had told him about it. "So my wife says."

Larky Nolson was doing more than just nod to Detective Inspector Sloan now. He was getting up from his seat beside Mrs. Nolson and coming over. Sloan, too, rose to his feet and then carefully made his way to a square of open space behind the clinic waiting area. Choosing your own ground was something you learned to do early on when you went on the beat. It was half-way towards winning.

Larky Nolson, however, had not come to do battle.

"Long time no see, Inspector," he began.

"That, Larky," responded Sloan easily, "is quite all right with me."

"Too long," said the little man meaningfully.

"I can bear it."

"Don't be like that."

"The longer the better," said Sloan firmly. That, in essence, had been the sentiment prevailing in the Crown Court too.

"That man . . ." Larky sucked his teeth.

"Which man?"

"Called hisself a judge."

"A good one."

"Him a judge!" said Larky richly. "He wouldn't even know which way was up."

"Black from white," declared Sloan. "That's all he needs to know."

Larky sniffed. "And the lawyers were no better."

"They're not in it for their health," said Sloan obliquely.

"You can say that again," said Larky indignantly. "And there wasn't much to choose between them if you ask me—mine or theirs."

"The legal profession's duty," recited Sloan piously, "is to the court."

"You'd have thought though," grumbled Nolson, ignoring this, "that mine could have got me less than he did."

"With your record?"

"If he was half as clever as he thought he was I'd have been a free man."

"I expect he knows a villain when he sees one."

"The other brief didn't help either. Your man."

"He isn't meant to," Sloan reminded him. "He's there to prosecute."

"Persecute, more like. Real nasty, I thought he was. Where did you get him from? The Kremlin or somewhere?"

"Too many short sentences about," said Sloan briskly.

"He made it all sound so much worse," persisted the burglar.

"Safes don't fall open on their own," observed the policeman.

The safe was a sore point with Larky. It had been difficult to open and that had been his undoing. He changed his ground.

"That your wife you're with over there?"

"It isn't anyone else's," said Sloan evenly.

"Your first?" enquired Nolson.

"Yes, as it happens it is."

"They're the worst," said Larky patronisingly.

"Are they?"

"Didn't think," sniffed Nolson, gaining strength, "that I'd ever see you here, Inspector."

"Say that again, Larky, and I'll hit you."

"Another little copper on the way." He rolled his eyes. "Give me strength."

"Causing an affray," said Sloan, moving forward irately. "That's what I'll get you for, Nolson. . . ."

The little man backed away. "It's as quiet as houses, Inspector. Honest . . ."

It wasn't as quiet as anything.

Hospitals were never quiet. And never still. At that moment the turgid procedure of the outpatient clinic produced a movement. A sister appeared and a woman disappeared through a door. Both men looked back towards their wives.

"I'm next," muttered Larky inappropriately.

Sloan started to make his way back to his own wife's side. He was diverted by the sight of another face he knew.

Dr. Dabbe was consultant pathologist to the Berebury District Hospital Management Committee. He was also police surgeon to the Berebury Division Police Force.

"Ah, Sloan, there you are."

"Good afternoon, Doctor."

The pathologist looked past Sloan and along the rows of heavily pregnant waiting patients, murmuring under his breath, *"Abou ben Adhem* [May His Tribe Increase]." He picked out Mrs. Sloan and waved to her.

"They said I'd find you here, Sloan."

"Did they?" said Sloan impassively.

"You're wanted," said Dr. Dabbe.

"Where?"

"Here."

"In the hospital?"

"Yes," said the pathologist.

"Oh, I am, am I?" began Sloan.

"Come along, man . . ."

"Who wants me?"

"I do, of course," said Dabbe impatiently.

"Where?"

"In the mortuary. Really, Sloan, I haven't got all afternoon to waste."

Neither had Sloan. He stood indecisively between his wife and the police surgeon. Margaret Sloan was giving him a look quite as enigmatic as that of the Mona Lisa. . . .

"There's no time to hang about," said the doctor. "Mortons are already on their way now."

Then Margaret Sloan raised her hand in an ironic gesture of absolution. Detective Inspector Sloan, a free man now, turned to the pathologist and said with alacrity, "Which way?"

* * *

The mortuary was on the ground floor of the hospital and admission from the outside world was by way of two sets of double doors. The outer set kept the curious at bay. The inner pair led to the mortuary itself.

By the time Dr. Dabbe and Detective Inspector Sloan reached the department a vehicle was already neatly sandwiched between the two sets of doors—looking for all the world like a barge trapped between lock gates on a canal.

A plump young man clambered out of the driver's seat as they approached. He nodded to the mortuary attendant and then gave the engine bonnet an affectionate slap.

"Nice, isn't it?" he said to the world at large.

"Very, Fred," said Sloan.

And it was. As an undertaker's van it was a masterpiece of both strict convention and ambiguity.

"We've just taken delivery," said Fred Morton proudly. "It's the latest thing."

It was white—like an ambulance—and indeed had two red crosses on the smoked darkly opaque windows of the rear double doors but there was also a precautionary black stripe running round the white walls, pointing a warning note. The neighbours would learn nothing from a visit of a van like this. Only the cognoscenti—the police, the fire people, real ambulancemen—would know what to make of it and its cargo.

"I said to Dad that we've got to move with the times. . . ."

"I remember," remarked Dr. Dabbe, "your father saying that to his father."

"We've still got that hearse," said young Morton reverently. "You can't touch Rolls-Royces. Fitted into the stable a treat, of course, otherwise Grandad would never have had it."

Morton and Son, Undertakers; Nethergate, Berebury, went back a long time.

Fred Morton moved around to open the rear doors. "There's one thing Dad won't let go, though."

"What's that?" asked Sloan curiously. Undertaking was a conservative trade and Morton and Son were more conservative than most.

"The sign above the shop." He sighed. "I just can't get Dad to change it for all that it doesn't make sense."

"What does it say?"

"Superior Funerals!" He groaned. "In black and gold lettering with scrolls—I ask you." He opened both the van doors as he spoke. "Here you are, Doctor. Beatrice Gwendoline Wansdyke."

"And what, exactly," enquired Sloan as he walked into the mortuary proper with the pathologist, "did Beatrice Gwendoline Wansdyke die from?"

"Diabetes," said Dr. Dabbe. "Or so I am told."

"And?"

"And nothing," said Dr. Dabbe blandly, "unless I find something else as well."

"So what's the problem?"

"The problem," said Dr. Dabbe, "is not so much what she died from as what she died with, if you see what I mean."

"No," said Sloan uncompromisingly, "I don't see what you mean. What did she die with?"

"A quarter of a million pounds," said the doctor.

Chapter 2

Sharp was the hope and hard the supposition.

"A quarter of a million pounds," said Superintendent Leeyes flatly. "That's what I told the doctor."

Sloan was in the mortuary office using the pathologist's secretary's telephone to ring the police station.

"Just sitting there," said Leeyes. "Doing nothing."

"Sitting where?" asked Sloan. As assorted bank and train robbers had found to their discomfiture, money of that order of magnitude took up a lot of space.

"In her bank account."

"Not under the bed or anything like that?"

"Nothing like that," said Leeyes firmly. "In her bank account. That's how we heard about it."

"From the bank?" said Sloan startled.

"No, no," said Leeyes. "Well, not exactly."

Sloan waited for enlightenment.

"Constable Blake's wife," said Leeyes, "overheard two young girls—bank clerks, actually—talking in the check-out queue at the supermarket yesterday dinnertime."

"Ah."

"Says one to the other, 'Fancy dying with a quarter of a million pounds in the bank.'" Leeyes grunted. " 'Before you can enjoy it,' says the other. 'Shame, isn't it? Mind you, she was old. . . .' Those were their words, Sloan."

"Then what?"

"Mrs. Blake—smart woman, Mrs. Blake . . ."

"Used to be in the force. Before she married Ted."

11

"Ah, that explains it. Well, she tails the pair of them . . ."

"Back to the bank?"

"Precisely. And we set about finding out who died yesterday. Only Miss Wansdyke."

Sloan cleared his throat. "There's no word out about any job of that size unaccounted for, is there, sir?"

"Not that I know of," replied Leeyes. "I've got someone down here at the station going through the back numbers now to be on the safe side all the same."

"It's a lot of money," he said warily.

"Better than Brink's," said Leeyes.

"Quite so," said Sloan, acknowledging this.

Every policeman had his own choice crime that he mulled over in much the same way as a connoisseur swirled his wine around in a glass to get the best of the bouquet. The Brink's Incorporated job in Boston was the one that continued to fascinate Superintendent Leeyes. Done by small-time men, he never failed to remind them. And that hadn't stopped it being the most daring bank robbery in history.

"That was in dollars, of course," added Leeyes now.

Sloan coughed. "It's not exactly a crime—er—in itself, so to speak, sir, to have that much money in the bank."

"It may not be," said Leeyes robustly, "but you must admit, Sloan, it's a bit funny for someone who lives in Ridley Road."

"It's very respectable up there," conceded Sloan.

"Exactly," said Leeyes, who beyond a certain point did not equate money with respectability. Not new money, that is. In the superintendent's book His Grace the Duke of Calleshire could have as much as he liked. That was different.

"In fact," persisted Sloan, "my wife would like us to think of moving that way now that . . ." He felt a pang of unease when he remembered his wife. Was she still sitting in the clinic, he wondered, or had she moved forward on the ante-natal conveyor belt?

Leeyes grunted. "A nice quiet neighborhood."

"Decent houses."

"Trees on the footpath."

"No through traffic," said Sloan.

"Grass verges," said Leeyes.

"Just local vehicles." Policemen grew to dislike cars.

"Near the tennis club."

"Good gardens, too, sir." Sloan's own recreation was growing roses. It was about the only one that went with his sort of working hours. "Clay soil."

"No trouble up there either." The superintendent added the ultimate police accolade.

"Not even on Saturday nights," said Sloan, completing the sketch of suburban delight. A Town and Country Planning Conference on urban housing amenity would have taken two days to get as far.

"See what I mean?" demanded Leeyes illogically. "What would someone living up in Ridley Road be doing with that much money?"

Sloan let the vision of him and his wife taking possession of a house in Ridley Road fade and said he didn't know. "Though there's always the football pools, sir," he said. "She might have said 'No publicity' to them and meant it. Some people do."

"First thing we checked," grunted Leeyes. "I don't know about you, Sloan, but it's the only way I can think of of getting your hands on that much money straight."

"Sad but true . . ."

"It is a melancholy indictment of modern society," intoned the superintendent in his best Watch Committee manner, "that gambling seems to be the only honest path to financial glory."

"Inheritance?" put in Sloan quickly before the superintendent could hit his full oratorical style.

"Rich uncles, you mean?" Leeyes paused. "That's a thought. I could put someone onto checking on big wills."

"They would have had to have been very rich uncles indeed," pointed out Sloan, "to have left that sort of money net."

"Oil-rich uncles?" postulated Leeyes. That this was another melancholy indictment of modern society seemed—for the moment—to have escaped him.

"Sugar daddy?" suggested Sloan, seeing that they were exploring arcane relationships.

"She was a bit long in the tooth for that sort of thing," said Leeyes.

"Ah." Sloan pulled his notebook towards him. He had all the policeman's desire for positive fact in an uncertain world. "How old exactly?"

"Fifty-nine," said Leeyes promptly. "She was due to retire next year."

"What from?"

"Didn't I tell you?" said Leeyes. "She was the chemistry mistress at the girls' grammar school here in Berebury."

"Why?"

"Why what, Sloan?" he snapped testily.

"Why was she working?" said Sloan not unreasonably. "If I had a quarter of a million pounds in the bank I shouldn't be working. Would you, sir?"

"Another hundred and sometimes I think I'd stop," said Leeyes forcefully. "Today's been murder. Harpe's got himself tangled up with a pack of rapid conservationists—Malcolm Darnley's crowd—at a county planning enquiry over some trees on a bend in the Calleford Road. Haven't seen hair or hide of him all day and we've had three road traffic accidents already not to mention that Dr. McCavity's hit another bollard. That's his third this month."

"Chemistry mistress at . . ." began Sloan. Dr. McCavity was old Dr. Paston's new partner and visibly inclined to the bottle. His patients, however, liked him.

"Sergeant Gelven's over at Almstone looking at a break-in and if you ask me that's about all he's going to be able to do to it."

"Chemistry mistress at the grammar school," said Sloan resolutely.

"Kennedy's gone and got his foot trodden on by a bull down at the market." Leeyes believed in airing his grievances to his subordinates—it kept their ambition within bounds. "He's up at the hospital, too. And Constable King's on annual leave. He would be, just when he's wanted. . . ." Police Constable King routinely acted as coroner's officer in Berebury.

"Yes, sir. You . . ."

"You've taken half a day's leave."

Sloan drew breath, remembered that he hadn't got a quarter of a million pounds in the bank or anywhere else, and kept silent.

"And Crosby's underfoot here," said Leeyes, concluding his catalogue of woe by piling Pelion upon Ossa. Detective Constable Crosby was not the brightest of the bright and tended to still be at the police station when other members of the force were out on the job.

"So," said Sloan, "what you want to know is . . ."

"What I want to know," said Superintendent Leeyes, defining the problem neatly, "is exactly what a quarter of a million pounds is doing in the current account of Beatrice Wansdyke."

"Who died?"

"What's that, Sloan?" came his voice sharply over the line. "What's that?"

"The late Beatrice Wansdyke," observed Sloan pertinently.

"Exactly!" trumpeted Leeyes. "Dying must come into it somewhere."

"It usually does," said Sloan, putting down the telephone receiver.

* * *

Sloan put his head outside the pathologist's secretary's office door and said, "You can have your office back now. Thank you."

"Oh, there you are, Inspector." The secretary was standing in the corridor talking to a young girl in nurse's uniform.

"There was a message," the girl was saying breathlessly.

"You are . . ." began the secretary.

"Nurse Petforth." The girl looked anxiously first at her and then at Detective Inspector Sloan. "I came as quickly as I could."

"Miss Briony Petforth?" said the secretary.

She nodded, whey-faced. "Sister said to come straight round here but she didn't say why. . . . Is it

. . ." She halted in mid-sentence and made a visible effort to control herself. "It's not . . . who . . . ?"

"Would you by any chance be a relative of the late Miss Beatrice Wansdyke?"

"Oh, yes." A look of great relief passed over the girl's face. "She was my aunt."

"Then," said the pathologist's secretary briskly, "that's what the message will have been about."

An expression of puzzlement succeeded relief on Miss Petforth's countenance. "But she died on Sunday. At least we think it must have been on Sunday."

"Dr. Dabbe," said Dr. Dabbe's secretary, "wants to do a postmortem and we find that there's been no formal identification."

"A postmortem? But I thought . . ." She pushed back a lock of auburn hair that had somehow found its way past her nurse's cap. "Dr. Paston said . . ."

"Only if you don't mind," said the pathologist's secretary, "of course."

"I don't mind," said Briony Petforth in such a neutral way that Detective Inspector Sloan was quite unable to make up his mind whether she did or not. "It's just that my cousin's been seeing to everything."

"Yes, indeed." The pathologist's secretary conjured up some papers. "That would be Mr. Bertram George Wansdyke, wouldn't it?"

"He's her executor," responded the nurse obliquely.

"We did try to get in touch with him," said the secretary, "at his firm."

"Wansdyke and Darnley."

"But he's over in Calleford on business all day," said Dr. Dabbe's secretary, "that's why the doctor thought that as you were on the spot and as it would save so much time . . ."

"The funeral's been arranged," said the girl. A certain amount of colour had come back into her face now.

"Yes, indeed." If the pathologist's secretary was very well aware that postmortems took a certain precedence over funerals she did not say so. "For next Saturday, isn't it?"

"That was for the school," Briony Petforth said. "It's

to be on Saturday morning so that the girls themselves can choose whether they come or not. Not to have it thrust upon them compulsorily."

"How very thoughtful."

"That was my cousin's idea."

Once again Sloan was unable to decide what Briony Petforth herself thought of it.

The pathologist's secretary was gathering up her papers. "So, Miss Petforth, if you would just come this way . . ."

Briony Petforth did not move.

"Dr. Paston," she said instead, "gave us—the family, that is—a death certificate when . . . when . . . after she was found. . . ."

"Did he?" The pathologist's secretary turned to her file. "Then I may have it here."

"He put down hyperglycemia and diabetic keto-acidosis as the cause of death," said the girl. "I saw it."

"Oh, yes?" The pathologist's secretary might have been a member of the medical profession herself, so skilled was she in parrying questions.

"She was diabetic, you see." Briony Petforth had now succeeded in getting the stray tail of auburn hair back under her cap.

"Bad luck," said the pathologist's secretary sympathetically.

"Had been for years."

"Such a lot of it about, too, these days. Now, if you would just come this way please . . ."

"So why," asked Briony Petforth, "is there being a postmortem?"

* * *

Someone else in Berebury was at that minute asking the very same question of someone quite different.

"How should I know?" responded George Wansdyke at the other end of a telephone in Calleford, the county town of Calleshire. "All I had was that message to the office asking if I was available this afternoon and naturally they said I wasn't, because I was over here in Calleford. We've had this appointment with the director of United Mellemetics' Research and Development Department lined up for weeks now and with Malcolm being away until Thursday . . ."

"But," his wife cut him off short, "you told me that Dr. Paston gave you a death certificate." Mrs. Wansdyke never encouraged mention of business detail. In fact she spent quite a lot of time trying to pretend to herself and her circle of friends and relations that her husband wasn't actually in anything so commonplace as business at all. Messrs. Wansdyke and Darnley, she was wont to insist, were really more like scientific researchers than plastics manufacturers.

"So he did," said George Wansdyke. "Yesterday."

"Well, then . . ."

"And it said something which he told me meant that she'd gone into a diabetic coma."

"That's doctors for you all the time," said Mrs. Pauline Wansdyke, momentarily diverted. "Dressing everything up in words nobody can understand. Why couldn't he say what he meant?"

"He did," said her husband mildly.

"Your aunt died from her diabetes. . . ."

"And that's exactly what he put on the death certificate," said George Wansdyke.

"In Latin, though," his wife came back at him swiftly.

"They all do that." In Greek actually, but he did not say so.

"Showing off," pronounced Mrs. Pauline Wansdyke. George did not argue.

Mrs. Wansdyke returned like a homing pigeon to her original point. "They can't do a post-mortem if they've got the death certificate."

"Can't they just!" responded George vigorously.

"Well, can they?"

"I don't suppose for one moment," declared George Wansdyke, businessman, "that they are doing anything at all that they haven't the authority to do." A working life spent—as a first priority—in satisfying an assortment of government departments, the Customs and Excise, the Inland Revenue, sundry local authorities, the Patents Office, and the Value Added Tax Commission-

ers had taught him only too well that there was invariably the power packed behind the punch. It was only in
the jungle of private enterprise that you had to make
sure first that you could see the colour of the other person's money, so to speak.

"But . . ." began Pauline Wansdyke.

"These sorts of people," he said ruefully, "don't need
to exceed their authority. They've got all they need and
plenty more where that came from. For all I know the
coroner can still clap people in the Tower."

"The coroner?" murmured Pauline Wansdyke.
"What's your aunt got to do with the coroner?"

"Nothing that I know about," said George grimly.
"Yet."

"Well then why should he want to put anyone in the
Tower?"

"What I meant was," explained George, immediately
regretting his flight into imagery, "that it seems to me
that the coroner in England can do pretty well what he
likes."

"Oh, I see, George. . . ." Pauline Wansdyke made
up in pertinacity what she lacked in comprehension.

"Yes?"

"Where does the coroner come in then?"

"Someone must have asked him for a post-mortem."

"Not you?"

"Not me," said George Wansdyke. "And I'm her sole
executor."

"Briony wouldn't have done, surely?"

"No, not without telling me. Anyway, she's a nurse
and she was sure that Beatrice had died of her diabetes."

"I know. She said so straightaway yesterday. So why
all the fuss if they know already?"

"You don't seem to have got the point yet," said
George tightly. "It isn't the medical people being in academic doubt about the cause of death and wanting to
find out so that everything's neat and tidy."

"No?"

"No," said George. "Otherwise they'd have asked
our permission for a post-mortem."

"Oh . . ."

"Someone's got the coroner to order one, which is a different kettle of fish altogether."

"Who would do that?"

"I don't know," said George Wansdyke, "but I'm certainly going to find out."

"Wait a minute," said Pauline.

"I know what you're going to say."

"Nicholas?"

"I wouldn't put it past him," said George Wansdyke.

"I wouldn't put anything past him," said Pauline spitefully. "Anything at all."

"No," said George.

"Nicholas Petforth," said Pauline, rolling the words around her tongue.

"Another name for trouble," he said ironically.

"No sense of family at all," said Mrs. Wansdyke, who had been a Miss Hartley-Powell before her marriage and never forgot it.

"He's not going to be buried in the family grave when his time comes," said George vigorously. "Not if I have any say in the matter."

"Oh," said Mrs. Wansdyke, whose attention span was not a long one, "that reminds me. Morton's rang to say that they were arranging to open the grave up as planned on Friday."

"Good," said George absently. "We'll see about bringing the stone up to date afterwards."

"I wonder if he'll come to the funeral on Saturday," said Pauline.

"Who?"

"Nicholas, of course. He always said he was fond of his aunt."

"Actions speak louder than words," said George Wansdyke. "We'll just have to wait and see, won't we?"

"He'll come," forecast Pauline Wansdyke with conviction. "For sure. You see if he doesn't."

"If he's still got a suit to his back."

Chapter 3

Although the devil didn't show his face
I'm pretty sure he was about the place.

The funeral of Beatrice Wansdyke was the last thing on the mind of Detective Inspector Sloan as he followed the pathologist through the mortuary doors into the dissecting room proper. In police measurement terms next Saturday and a funeral was a very long way away from this Tuesday and a post-mortem. A week was a long time in other things besides politics.

Dr. Dabbe was soon struggling into gown and rubber apron. He was helped in this exercise by his assistant, a perennially silent man called Burns.

"There's one thing, Sloan," said the pathologist, busily rolling up his sleeves.

"Yes?"

"The dibs don't show here, do they?"

"No, Doctor." Sloan was the first to agree with that. Nothing of this world's goods showed in the post-mortem room.

The pathologist, gowned now, moved over towards the dissecting table and ran his eyes over the body. "No external signs of violence immediately visible," he murmured. "I haven't missed any gunshot wounds, have I, Burns?"

"No, Doctor," said the assistant, adding, deadpan, "not yet."

This was evidently a private joke between master and man.

"Nor a stab in the back?"

"The back has not been stabbed," said Burns.

"That leaves the field clear to begin then," said Dabbe easily. He reached up and adjusted a small microphone hanging a little way above the post-mortem table. "Are you there, Rita? We're ready now."

The voice of the pathologist's secretary came back to them through some unobtrusive intercom. "I'm here, Doctor. Carry on."

"Body of an averagely nourished female," Dr. Dabbe began dictating, "whose age has been given to me as fifty-nine and whose name I am told is Beatrice Gwendoline Wansdyke."

The voice of the secretary broke in. "She's been positively identified, Doctor, now. By her niece."

The pathologist nodded and began peering forward at a wide area of thickened skin at the front of the dead woman's right thigh. He spoke into the hanging microphone again. "No external signs of violence except that there are indications that subcutaneous injections have been given over a long period."

"That's the diabetes, I suppose," said Sloan. What the police meant by violence was quite clearly something very different from that which the pathologist meant by violence.

"It's funny," mused the doctor, "how all the old diabetic hands find one site and use it all the time for their injections."

"Rather them than me," said Sloan.

"They've plenty of places to choose from," said Dabbe, "yet they usually find the one and stick to it."

"Does her choosing her right thigh mean she was right-handed?" asked Sloan. Anything that he could find out about Beatrice Wansdyke to add to his meagre store of information might be a help: you never knew with police work.

"I should think so," said Dabbe. He ran a professional eye over two biceps muscles. "You can take it from me that the deceased was right-handed anyway."

Sloan wrote that down. It was a beginning.

"Right, then," said the pathologist cheerfully, "shall we go in headfirst?"

Sloan stood well back. The hanging microphone

looked like the spider descending beside little Miss
Muffet. . . .

"The deep end, you might say," murmured Dr.
Dabbe as Burns busied himself with a stainless-steel
knife.

"Beg pardon, Doctor?" In Detective Inspector
Sloan's considered view this was neither the time nor
the place to be playing with words.

"She was educated, wasn't she? Miss Wansdyke . . ."

"What . . . oh, yes. A science degree." That, too,
had—like the quarter of a million pounds—been left
behind outside the post-mortem room. This world's
goods were not the only things that did not show up
here. University degrees didn't carry any weight either.
How right the ancients had been to drape what they
were pleased to call achievements round the tomb instead. . . .

A wicked-looking bone saw had succeeded the knife
in Burns' hand.

Sloan stirred. "What are you looking for, Doctor?"

"Cause of death, old chap. Nothing less, nothing
more." He peered over his assistant's shoulder at the
late Miss Wansdyke's head. "Looks all right to me."

"Yes, Doctor," said Burns.

The pathologist turned towards the hanging microphone and translated this for his secretary into medico-
legal English for his report. "No macroscopic changes
in brain tissue."

Presently: "Rita, are you still there?"

"Yes, Doctor, I'm here."

"No signs of strangulation. All the larynx bones are
intact—hyoid and all."

Then: "Lungs normal. Got that?"

"Yes, Doctor."

A little later: "Some signs of myocardial degenera-
tion. You'd expect that, of course."

And quite quickly after that: "Minimal diabetic
changes in the pancreas. Bound to be with her history, I
suppose. We'll have all the usual tissue sections, Burns,
please. Rita, do a list, will you?"

"Yes, Doctor."

"And put the kettle on."

Detective Inspector Sloan had never relished post-mortems and he didn't enjoy this one now. Neverthe-less, as always, there was something quite fascinating about watching a true expert at work. Gradually simple atavistic distaste fell away. It was succeeded by some-thing much less primitive. The pathologist must have sensed his interest because he shot the policeman a shrewd glance and said: "You're quite right to take your shoes off, Sloan."

He started. "Beg pardon, Doctor?"

"Metaphorically, of course."

"I don't see . . ."

"You're in the Temple of Truth now," said the doc-tor drily. "As well as inside Nature's Temple."

"Oh?"

"The human body."

"Ah, I see what you mean."

"The greatest creation of them all," said the patholo-gist soberly. "Don't make any mistake about that, Sloan."

"No, Doctor."

"All alike and none exactly the same into the bar-gain."

"I hadn't thought about that."

"Mathematicians"—the pathologist waved a rubber-gloved hand—"contemplate infinity."

"Do they?"

"I contemplate human dissimilarity."

Detective Inspector Sloan looked first at the patholo-gist, then at Burns, and then at the body on the post-mortem table. "We're all one-off models, are we then? The long and the short and the tall."

"We're all the same and we're all different," said Dr. Dabbe the specialist. "Past, present, and future. That's the wonder of it, Sloan, the sheer wonder . . ."

There was a sudden clatter near the mortuary door. At the same time over the intercom came the hasty voice of the pathologist's secretary. "Rita, here, Doctor. You've got a visitor. He said he'd been sent."

The door opened and a very young policeman stepped into the mortuary. At once the atmosphere changed from the philosophic to the mundane. The newcomer addressed himself first to Sloan.

"Detective Constable Crosby, sir, reporting for duty."

Sloan sighed. "Come in, Crosby."

"The superintendent said to step round, sir."

"Did he?"

"There wasn't anyone else."

"No."

"And . . ."

"And?"

"And he'd got word that the assistant chief constable might be dropping in to the station this afternoon."

"Ah." That explained the superintendent's eagerness to get Crosby out of it. "Get your notebook out then."

"Yes, sir." The constable struggled with a recalcitrant pocket and gave a greeting to the pathologist the while. "Afternoon, Dr. Dabbe." He nodded amiably to Burns and then his eye fell upon the body on the postmortem table. He moved over politely as if she, too, was of the gathering. "Hullo," he said, "it's Miss Wansdyke, isn't it?"

"I didn't know," said Sloan with heavy irony, "that you two knew each other. How come, Crosby?"

* * *

A telephone bell rang.

Technical progress has done a lot for the telephone bell. In business offices unobtrusive warbles, discreet flashing lights, or quiet buzzers draw attention to the instrument. In the Berebury District General Hospital where a little extra peace and quiet would not have come amiss it rang with old-fashioned clarity.

"Ante-natal outpatients' clinic," said the young nurse who answered it.

"This is Fleming Ward," said a voice. "Can I speak to Dr. Roger Elspin, please?"

"Is it urgent?" enquired the nurse. "He's seeing a patient at the moment."

"Penny, is that you? It's Briony here."

"Briony! What on earth's the matter?"

"Penny, I simply must speak to Roger this very minute."

"But he's in the clinic with a patient. Truly."

"If I come straight down will you let me in for a minute to see him?"

"What if Sister Stork catches you here?"

"She need never even know that I've been in her precious clinic."

"She'll know," declared Penny feelingly. "She always knows everything. Don't ask me how, though."

"I expect she's a witch really," said Briony Petforth with surprising matter-of-factness. "All hospital sisters are. In disguise. Look here, are you going to let me in or aren't you?"

"Well . . ."

"Only for a minute, I promise."

"Oh, all right then. . . ."

"I can say that I've come down with a message from Fleming Ward."

"And exactly what sort of message," demanded Penny with some spirit, "would a men's surgical ward have got for an obstetrics outfit?"

"I'll think of something on the way down," promised Briony Petforth. "You see if I don't."

"Mind, you'll have to wait until Sister Fleming's back's turned."

This seemed to go without saying and Briony Petforth rang off and sped down to the ante-natal clinic. Her friend, Penny, gave her a conspiratorial look.

"Now's your chance. Sister Stork's on the other phone to the delivery ward."

"Bless you," said Briony. "I won't forget this."

"Sister Stork will kill me if she ever finds out," declared Penny dramatically.

"Sister Fleming will kill me if she finds out," returned Briony more tersely. "I should be doing dressings."

"It must be important," said Penny, wide-eyed. "He's in the first consulting room on the right."

Briony tapped on the door.

"Let's see, it's Mrs. . . . Mrs. . . . er . . . Sloan,

isn't it?" the obstetrics registrar was saying to his patient.

"It is." Margaret Sloan had at last worked her way to the top of the queue in the clinic and a moment ago had actually been ushered into the medical presence. Her husband—in the way of police husbands—had not returned to her side before she did so, but Larky Nolson had waved to her as he and his wife had departed from the ante-natal clinic ahead of her.

It had been poor consolation.

"Let me see now," said the doctor in the manner of all doctors, "the baby's due pretty soon, isn't it?"

The knock on the door was repeated.

"Come in," commanded Dr. Elspin.

"Dr. Elspin," said Briony Petforth formally, "could you spare a moment, please?"

"Certainly, nurse." The obstetrics registrar paused in the act of reading Mrs. Margaret Sloan's case notes and excused himself to her.

Mrs. Sloan murmured, "Of course."

Dr. Elspin stepped with alacrity into the adjoining examination cubicle and abandoned his professional manner. "Darling, what's the matter?"

"Oh, Roger . . ."

"You look as if you've seen a ghost."

She laughed shakily. "Only poor Aunt Beatrice."

"Now," he began briskly, something of his professional manner coming back, "you must start forgetting all about that. I know you found her and that you were fond of her but . . ."

"Not that."

"No?"

"You don't understand, Roger. Something else."

"What?"

"They're doing a post-mortem."

"Well, why not? After all, old Paston has every right to request . . ."

"No." She shook her head impatiently. "You don't understand. He gave us the death certificate all right. It was after that. Roger, what would make them change their minds?"

The young doctor frowned and paused for a moment before he spoke. "I don't really know."

"There you are then."

"But there's no harm done. You should know that, darling. . . ."

"How do you know?" she demanded tightly.

Dr. Roger Elspin made no audible answer to this. Instead there was a silence.

It was not broken for a long minute.

No one has ever pretended that those screens and partition walls in hospitals which do not reach the floor and are of less than ceiling height are meant to be soundproof. They exist solely to give an illusion of privacy to the patient—nothing more. And in any case that illusion was only ever meant to extend to visual privacy. Nobody, unless completely deceived by the token aloneness of being behind screens, could really believe that speech and sound were protected in any way.

Or could they?

Mrs. Margaret Sloan, no ugly duckling herself in her day, reckoned that she knew what a kiss sounded like as well as the next woman.

"No, Roger," she heard Briony protest, "not here!"

"Why not?" mumbled Roger Elspin indistinctly.

"Roger, mind my cap. . . ."

Mrs. Sloan was even more sure of the sound the second time she heard it. The partition was, after all, only an aid to dignity—the patient's dignity.

"Roger, stop it! Sister might come in."

"And she might not," said the obstetrics registrar promptly. "Then look what I'd have missed."

"Roger, be serious for a minute."

"I am serious," retorted the young man.

"Roger, you musn't. . . ."

"Give me another kiss and I'll prove it."

"Darling." The timbre of her voice changed noticeably.

"You know very well," said Roger Elspin gruffly, "that I am serious."

"And you realise what this means?" said Briony urgently.

"Your Aunt Beatrice dying?"

"Yes." Briony Petforth let out a sigh that Mrs. Margaret Sloan heard quite clearly. "It means that now there is nothing in the whole world stopping us getting married."

Chapter 4

I give fair warning you may search for ever;
A golden future lures one on to sever
Oneself from all one ever had, and trust
An art for which one cannot lose the lust . . .

"How is it, Crosby," repeated Detective Inspector Sloan evenly, "that you happen to know Miss Wansdyke?"

Constable Crosby did not—in any sense—live anywhere near Ridley Road.

"She's the lady who lost her little dog," said the detective constable. "Very upset about it at the time, sir, she was."

"And what time would that have been exactly?" asked Sloan. Someone down at the police station had been detailed to teach Crosby about the more precise reporting of fact but they evidently hadn't got very far yet.

"Saturday, sir." He turned back the pages of his notebook. "Saturday morning. Miss Wansdyke asked if anyone had brought her dog in to us."

"And had they?"

"No, sir. I looked in the book and all we had that day was a budgerigar, two umbrellas, a slide rule, four scarves, and a stone of plain flour."

"But no dog?" The esoteric wonder of lost property had palled on Sloan long before he had left the beat.

"No, sir. No dog."

"What sort of dog?"

"A lady dog, sir."

Sloan took a deep breath and then said very gently, "What kind of dog, Crosby?"

"She said it answered to the name of Isolde, sir." He sounded doubtful.

"What happy breed?" enquired the pathologist helpfully. He was engaged in poring over some wicked-looking instruments.

"An Airedale, Doctor."

"Ah, short hair and long legs." Dr. Dabbe picked out something slender in stainless steel from those arrayed on a tray. "Could have upset the diabetes, of course."

"What could?" said Sloan.

"Losing her dog. Anxiety and distress—worry—too much of that sort of thing can throw a diabetic quite off balance." He indicated Burns, who was busily putting specimens from the postmortem into labelled jars. "We'll be doing the blood-sugar level anyway. That'll be a good guide."

"When did she lose her dog?" asked Sloan.

The detective constable turned back his notebook. "It wasn't there when she got home from school the day before she came in to us."

"Friday afternoon?"

"That's right, sir. She thought it must have got out of the house somehow while she was at school but that it would come back all right for the night."

"And it didn't?"

"No, sir. She said that she went out to look for it herself but she hadn't been feeling very well so she didn't go far."

Policeman and pathologist both looked up at that.

Dr. Dabbe spoke first. Medically. "She wouldn't have been feeling very well anyway if she was already on her way to a diabetic coma."

"But she didn't know how it was that the dog got out?" said Sloan, thinking quickly along quite another tack. A law-enforcement one.

"No, sir," said Crosby.

The pathologist shot the detective inspector a shrewd glance. "Have we the same thing in mind, Sloan?"

"Ransom?" responded Sloan.

"It's a growth industry." Dabbe waved an instrument in the air. "First cousin to sky-jacking."

"Children in Italy . . ." It was something, he supposed, that there were national traditions in crime, and that Great Britain did not always lead the way.

"Dogs in England," said the pathologist, a cynic if ever there was one. "We're a nation of animal lovers."

"It might just have been an accident," said Sloan, "the dog getting out . . ."

"It is a truth universally acknowledged," said the doctor drily, "that a middle-aged woman in possession of a fortune will attract people anxious to part her from it."

Sloan coughed. "Would you say that an Airedale dog could be someone's—er—hostage to fortune?"

"Yes," said Dabbe simply.

"She was very upset," contributed Crosby, "especially when we told her that we hadn't got her—er—Isolde."

"We'll look for a note," conceded Sloan. "Just in case someone got ideas about ransom. Can't very well do more than that at this stage."

"No." The pathologist went back to his work and in a matter of moments was totally absorbed again in what he was doing. Detective Constable Crosby settled himself against a nearby bench while Sloan considered Miss Wansdyke and her curiously great wealth. It was some little time before Dr. Dabbe straightened up and began peeling off his rubber gloves. He continued, however, to address the microphone, which hovered—like Damocles' sword—above the neck of the post-mortem subject.

"Right, Rita. That's all. Get it typed out, will you, and I'll sign a copy for the coroner." He tossed his gloves into a linen basket. "It won't tell him much, Sloan."

"No?"

"I can't find anything except the diabetes." He turned his back on Sloan while his assistant, Burns, undid his gown from behind. "Of course she'd got the usual signs you'd expect to find going with that condition in a woman of her age."

"Change and decay?" Sloan's mother was a great churchgoer.

"Ever present, old chap, but no other cause of death

that I can see. Poison's always a problem though in forensic medicine."

"Yes, Doctor." And it was, too. That, as every policeman—and pathologist—knew, was where the undetected homicide lay. Nearly always.

"Naturally we'll take a look at the bits and pieces that Burns here has got in his jars," said Dabbe a trifle unscientifically, "but there are certainly no signs that lead me to suspect anything out of the ordinary in the way of what the lawyers call noxious substances."

Burns drew a white sheet up over the body of Beatrice Wansdyke.

"And no other natural causes," said Sloan, trying to keep his mind clear, "besides the diabetes."

"Just the diabetes," repeated the pathologist, tossing his gown into the linen basket after the gloves. "From my point of view there's no doubt at all what she died from even though someone somewhere may have smelt a rat."

"That's all right, Doctor," interrupted Detective Constable Crosby largely. He uncoiled himself from the bench against which he had been leaning. "After all, down at the station, we're in the rat-catching business, aren't we?"

* * *

Miss Simpson, headmistress of the Berebury Grammar School for Girls, picked up a piece of paper from her desk and studied it carefully. The deputy head of the school, Miss Walsh, had just brought it in to her study and laid it before her. The two women, seasoned schoolmistresses both, knew without discussion exactly how much burning of midnight oil the finished document represented.

It contained all the revisions in the school timetable made necessary by the sudden demise of the senior chemistry mistress.

Miss Simpson let it lie in her hands for a moment before she considered it, thinking instead of Beatrice Wansdyke. From now on someone else was going to have to persuade girls to think scientifically, to take a

proper interest in those twins of fundamental discovery,
Boyle and Charles and their laws, and to learn about
elements and atoms and (as far as Miss Simpson was
concerned—she was an English specialist herself) other
things.

Anyway, from now on another teacher of chemistry
was going to have to be categoric about nitric and ni-
trous and nitrate and somehow inculcate into her
charges the intellectual reaches opened up by the study
of organic chemistry.

Miss Wansdyke's syllabus would be up-to-date.
There wouldn't be any worry there. The upper sixth's
chances of university entrance would not be spoilt by
her death. They would suffer only by loss of contact
with a good mind. It had been a mind that had always
been ready and prepared to stretch the thinking of the
young. Girls who made sweeping statements once seldom made them a second time.

It had been much the same in the staff room. Col-
leagues who made unsupported assertions were apt to
have them challenged pretty speedily. Miss Simpson
sighed. Unfortunately staff-room politics seldom had
anything to do with principles—scientific or even first.

Miss Simpson let her eye fall on the timetable. Had
Miss Walsh . . . yes, she had. The head was not surprised to see that in her attempt to fill the gap in the
timetable the deputy head had slipped in a couple of
extra economics classes for the fifth form. Beatrice
Wansdyke wouldn't have liked that. As a scientist she
had always resented the intrusion of economics into the
curriculum as a separate subject. Economics, she maintained, was not a proper teaching entity at all, but an
ill-defined grey area, which knew no morality, somewhere between geography and history. And the proper
study of history, she was wont to parody Alexander
Pope, is power and if economics didn't come into that
she didn't know what did. A science, she would insist,
jealous of the purity of her own subject, it certainly was
not.

The aggrandisement of economics as a study apart,
though, thought Miss Simpson thankfully, Beatrice
Wansdyke would not have minded the waters closing so

quickly over the hole left by a departed chemistry mistress. The last thing she would have wanted was fuss. She would have thoroughly approved of the quiet rearrangement of the timetable and the stepping into her shoes of another teacher. The show, all dedicated pedagogues were agreed, must go on. Miss Collins would mind, of course. Hilda Collins and Beatrice Wansdyke had been good friends over the years—but then Hilda was a biologist and they were seldom sentimentalists.

The head paused in her thinking. She would have to decide herself whether to recommend to the governors that young Miss Peel should go up a rung in the academic ladder. A promising youngster, Miss Wansdyke had thought her. . . .

Mentally apologising to Beatrice's memory for meditating on her successor quite so soon, Miss Simpson was confronted by the thought that her late colleague had not been greatly looking forward to her retirement. Sitting back and resting was no fine ambition compared with the satisfaction of stretched elastic young minds. Better, too, to die while still searching for her own particular philosopher's stone.

Beatrice had been too much of a realist, too, she was sure, not to have observed the inevitable advances of old age, the decline in physical activity, the slow closing in of horizons that went with the passing years. Her manner had got more and more dry with the passage of time, though the girls whom she taught did not seem to mind. Miss Simpson smiled wryly to herself in the privacy of her study. There was no doubt that Beatrice Wansdyke had long ago reached that point in a schoolmistress's career when she was cherished by her pupils as much for her idiosyncrasy as her teaching.

The head laid the revised timetable back on her desk. No . . . Beatrice Wansdyke wouldn't have minded dying in harness, her duty done, her old friend Hilda Collins her chief mourner. She'd nursed her aged parents, kept her temper and her peace over the years with the silly snobbish brainless creature whom her brother's son had married, and done what she could for her dead sister's children. Nobody could have done more for the boy, Nicholas, than Beatrice, and who, added Miss Simpson charitably, could say yet that she had failed? He might improve and settle down in time. Who could say?

Would he, though, she wondered, come to the funeral on Saturday?

* * *

The young man who was the subject of Miss Simpson's thoughts was at that particular moment by no means as sure as Pauline Wansdyke had been that he would be at his aunt's funeral. This uncertainty had nothing to do with his wish to be there. It was to do with the nature and conditions of his present employment.

"No," the foreman was saying flatly, "you can't have next Saturday off."

"For a funeral," mumbled Nicholas Petforth.

The foreman, it transpired, had heard that one before. Many times.

"She was the only aunt I had," said Nicholas Petforth truthfully. That, though he didn't tell the foreman so, was the whole trouble in the family. Aunts had been a bit on the short side. His father had had no sisters and his mother only one. This situation didn't usually matter but it had mattered in their family when it came to the point. . . .

"And Saturday," said the foreman without emotion, "is the only time this season that Luston Town will be playing Newcastle United."

Nicholas Petforth's mobile face looked quite blank.

"Away," added the foreman meaningfully. "You'd need the whole day to get there. And"—he was a soured man—"and you'd be late back on Monday morning into the bargain."

"Ah, football." Petforth rearranged his features upon the instant to project a keen interest in the game. Negotiations about his going to the funeral had reached a delicate stage and he didn't want them spoilt by an injudicious reference on his part to spectator sport.

"Back late on Monday with a headache," added the foreman for good measure.

Petforth dragged up a remark he'd overheard being
made at a recent tea break. "The Town team haven't a
chance without their usual centre forward."

The foreman nodded. "Unluckiest accident in the
history of the club."

"And just before the big match," agreed Petforth solemnly. He became suitably deferential. "Do you think
if he'd been fit to play . . . supposing he hadn't broken his leg . . ."

The foreman shook his head. "Not a hope, if you ask
me."

"Ah . . ." Nicholas Petforth was careful not to
make a specific comment. He had learnt a lot since he
had come to work on the construction site. In his time
there he had come to perfect an ideal response to almost all remarks thrown at him. Boiled down, it consisted of inviting the speaker to agree with his or her
own last statement. It had proved a sure-fire way of
winning friends and influencing people. Sometimes he
threw in an additional "You've got a point there" for
good measure.

He did now.

"I know I have," declared the foreman. "Stands to
reason in a small club like Luston Town."

"True."

"This aunt of yours," said the foreman.

"More like a mother to me," said Petforth.

The foreman looked at him sharply.

The labourers he had under him these days weren't
like the ones he used to have. University students were
two-a-penny on the site nowadays, graduates almost as
common. They'd be having women heaving earth about
next, as the Russians did, and the Chinese—not that
some of the men around didn't look like women. He'd
got over thinking them all Maryannes though. There
just wasn't anyone around any more with the clout to
tell them to get their hair cut. And they weren't all fools
either. There had been a law graduate wanting to make
a quick penny to set himself up who had taught the
foreman himself a thing or two about questioning the
authority of those above him.

"Practically brought me up," offered the young man before him, whom the foreman knew only as Nick.

"No family?"

"Killed," said Petforth expressively, "in a pile-up on a motorway like this." He waved his hand to indicate the area they were working on. In fact at this early stage it bore no resemblance to a motorway at all. The three-lane landscaped tarmacadamed communications artery that was to come where they stood was little more than a twinkle in the planners' eye at this moment. In their minds' eye—and in the artist's impression—the well-intentioned road architects saw only the finished product—just as at Passchendaele the General Staff had visualised only victory. What the men on the ground saw in both cases was only mud.

"It happens," said the foreman.

"I was quite small at the time."

"Ah." That explained a lot to the foreman. Like why a well-spoken lad like this should be living in squalor and working with a road construction gang, though admittedly times had changed anyway. Time was when speech like his would have been aped up and down the site. Not any longer. The foreman reached for the last shot in his empty locker and said, "You'll lose your bonus, of course."

Nicholas Petforth shrugged his shoulders.

That didn't surprise the foreman. He couldn't get at any of his men that way any longer. The odd ones had minds above money and the others were earning so much that it didn't matter to them anyway.

In the end the foreman agreed to Nick having next Saturday off as he agreed to most requests these days. Partly because he didn't think for all his broken-down appearance and bizarre clothing that Nick Petforth was the sort of man to lie and partly because he calculated that he'd have the union after him if he didn't let him go. And then the consortium which was building the motorway and who would neither know nor care if he gave every manjack in the gang the whole week off, provided they didn't lose money, would be after his blood.

"You'll be back after the funeral, right?" he said,

conscious that if there was ever trouble on the site that he could be sure of just one thing: no one would ever uphold his authority.

"Not if she's left me a fortune, I won't," murmured the young man, picking up his donkey jacket and protective helmet. "That's for sure."

Chapter 5

If you would publish your infatuation
Come on and try your hand at transmutation.

"At least," murmured Mrs. Margaret Sloan, "I don't have to walk home."

"No," agreed Sloan warily. He'd gone straight back to the ante-natal outpatients' clinic from the mortuary and metaphorically thrown his hat in first.

There was a constrained silence.

"Everything—er—all right?" he asked.

"Yes," she said consideringly. "Yes, I think so."

"Good." He paused. "Er . . . good."

"If you're talking about the baby, that is."

"Yes . . . er . . . naturally."

"Then it is."

"Er . . . good."

"And me?"

"Of course," he said hastily. He'd fallen into that, headfirst.

There was another small silence.

"Is everything," Sloan capitulated, "all right with you too?"

"Yes, I think so," she said demurely.

"Good. Er . . . good. Here, let me take that."

Mrs. Sloan consented to having her shopping bag carried as they walked down the hospital corridor.

"The doctors are pleased then?" said her husband with unaccustomed heartiness and a wholesale avoidance of the equally germane matter of whether or not Mrs. Margaret Sloan was pleased at being abandoned in the ante-natal clinic.

"The doctor," said Margaret Sloan astringently, "was very pleased indeed."

"Good. I'm glad to hear it."

"But not with me."

Sloan looked up.

"He," said Margaret Sloan, matron, "was pleased with a young lady called Briony."

"Ah, he was, was he?"

"Exceedingly pleased. Mind you," she added, "Dr. Elspin is what I would call a very personable young man."

Somehow this statement contrived to put Sloan on the wrong foot.

"Would you?" he said.

"Very," said Margaret Sloan emphatically.

"Ah!"

"Nice manners."

"Has he?"

"For a doctor," she said.

"I see."

"And you," she said, "presumably were—er—caught up with someone called Beatrice?"

"I was," said Sloan carefully. The Ice Maiden was gradually—but ever so gradually—giving way to someone else—someone more like the woman he had married. He didn't want to say or to do anything that might halt the progression.

"Aunt to a nurse called Briony, I take it?" said his wife.

"That is so. The late Miss Beatrice Wansdyke. I understand that she has a niece on the staff at the hospital."

"If," said Mrs. Sloan, "what I overheard is anything to go by . . ."

"Yes?"

"She's going to have a nephew on the staff at the hospital too pretty soon."

"Ah."

"A nephew-in-law, actually."

"I see." He listened attentively to her recital of what she had overheard. "So now they can get married and before she died they couldn't?"

"That was what was implied certainly," said Mrs. Margaret Sloan.

"Well, well, well," said Sloan, "that is interesting."

"I rather thought," murmured his wife mischievously, "that you wouldn't think I'd been wasting my time."

"Margaret Sloan," he said gruffly, "I won't have that from you or anyone else." He took a quick look up and down the corridor. They seemed for the moment to be alone. He dropped the shopping basket and put both arms around her. He was delighted to find that the Ice Maiden had melted away completely.

"Larky Nolson waved to me," she said indistinctly.

"I'll have him for that," swore Sloan.

"It's not a crime."

"Incitement to violence," growled Margaret Sloan's husband, "that's what that was."

An Accident Unit porter wheeling a patient on a stretcher trolley around the corner at that moment rolled his eyes and said to his mate at tea-break time that the young doctors were bad enough these days but he really didn't know what the police force was coming to.

* * *

To say that Superintendent Leeyes was displeased by the news of the result of the post-mortem examination was an understatement.

Detective Inspector Sloan was sitting in the superintendent's office now. There had been a tacit—definitely unspoken—agreement between police husband and policeman's wife that he was going back on duty.

Leeyes was inveighing against all forensic scientists in general but medical ones in particular.

"It's always the same with pathologists," he complained. "When you don't want them to find something they go and do, and when you do want them to come up with the goods they don't."

Sloan maintained a prudent silence. Abstract truth was not a concept that appealed to the superintendent at the best of times. And this was not the best of times.

While it was not the worst of times either, it did not seem as if the superintendent considered it was the age of medical wisdom.

"So Miss Wansdyke died of her diabetes, did she?" he rumbled after a moment. Perhaps it was the epoch of incredulity.

"Dr. Dabbe couldn't find anything else, sir."

"He would if he could," conceded Leeyes illogically.

"He's doing a drug screen, of course."

"Of course." That went without saying. Drug screens were routine in this day and age.

"They may discover something in some of the other specimens they've taken."

"Disappointing there being nothing to find at autopsy." Leeyes grunted. "I should have thought there was bound to be more to her dying than natural causes."

"Seems a pity to die with all that money," Sloan agreed with the unspoken sentiment and then added a witticism of his own. "All this and heaven too."

"Something doesn't fit, Sloan," said the superintendent severely.

"No, sir." Sloan was quick to agree.

"Doesn't feel right."

"No, sir," he said immediately. He didn't discount instinct. He never had. Hunch was halfway to detection. Always had been.

"Doesn't smell right either," pronounced Leeyes.

"No, sir." You used all your senses in police work.

"On the other hand I don't see that we can do a lot more about holding things up."

"No."

"So," said Leeyes generously, "you can just step round and tell the coroner we shan't be standing in his way at all any more over the burial order."

*   *   *

His office was not the only thing Dickensian about Mr. Robert Chestley. He was one of Her Majesty's coroners for the county of Calleshire and a practising solicitor. The man himself gave the impression of barely having left a hard butterfly-wing collar behind. A gold-rimmed pince-nez contributed to a general aura of the nineteenth century, which was reinforced by the decor of an office in which little had been changed since his grandfather's day.

Detective Inspector Sloan was not deceived.

Unseen legal scale fees kept pace with the rise in the cost of living practically of their own volition. There was no need for any other changes.

"You," said Mr. Chestley, notary public and no-body's fool, "have come about the late Miss Beatrice Wansdyke."

Sloan agreed that he had.

"Constable King's away," grumbled the coroner. Mr. Chestley himself never took holidays. "He usually sees to everything."

Sloan concurred with that too. They were all agreed that the coroner's officer was a useful man to have around at a death. He saved the beatman a lot of routine work, devilled for the coroner, and became—thank goodness—very skilled indeed at handling bereaved relatives.

"Your superintendent," said the coroner with emphasis, "prevailed upon me to order a post-mortem examination."

He and Superintendent Leeyes were old adversaries. They had had several notable clashes in the past—usually over the duties of the coroner's officer. This unfortunate policeman existed in a sort of leaderless no-man's-land. Hostilities had broken out over this more than once.

"Subject to my direction," the superintendent always insisted.

"Subject to my direction," the coroner would invariably counter.

"His office derives from the parish beadle," Mr. Chestley would reply, "and that's older. My pigeon, I think."

"Historical duties too obscure to be recorded," said Leeyes nastily on more than one occasion. The ancientness of the coroner's own office always rankled with him. Sir Robert Peel had been so unconscionably late on the scene.

"Jervis on Coroners . . ."

"The Police Act 1964 . . ." Superintendent Leeyes never gave up.

"Useful to have a police officer around in case a crime has been committed," would throw in the coroner.

"If you need a detective," Leeyes always came back smartly at that one, "we'll send one round."

"The job calls for a trained man." The coroner—a pillar of the legal profession—always had a riposte for every rebuttal.

"Waste of police manpower" had figured in Leeyes's broadside in response to that.

"If a job is worth doing," quoted Chestley, "then it's worth doing well."

"No man can serve two masters." Leeyes did not hesitate to fall back on primary sources when it suited him.

Then someone—the chief constable probably—had called "Pax" and a state of armed neutrality had been resumed.

"So," said Mr. Chestley to Detective Inspector Sloan now, "I ordered a post-mortem, the body being within my jurisdiction."

"Yes," said Sloan. It was the latter point that mattered with coroners, though he never knew why.

"That post-mortem examination confirms the cause of death as certified by the deceased's usual medical attendant."

"Yes," said Sloan again.

"Can you now give me any valid reason why I should not issue a Pink Form B?"

"No," said Sloan uneasily.

"I take it, Inspector, that Superintendent Leeyes had felt—er—a pricking of his thumbs."

"Information received," said Sloan tersely. Formal language was a refuge really, not an imposition: a cloak for that which was better not explained. "From persons about the deceased." The quaint archaism covered a multitude of hidden sources.

"Pink Form B," expounded the coroner pedantically, "is of course a superior category of medical certificate of the cause of death."

"Yes," said Sloan, surprised at the law's homely touch. Down at the police station forms had numbers, not colours and letters.

"Though," Mr. Chestley continued his lecture, "as it happens the result of the autopsy confirms the cause of death as certified by the registered medical practitioner who attended the deceased in her last illness."

"Dr. Paston," said Sloan for simplicity's sake.

"The fact of confirmation is irrelevant," continued the coroner, adjusting his pince-nez.

Not in Sloan's mind, it wasn't, though he did not say so. "Corroboration" was the word the police used for that and they could always use as much of it as they could get in the criminal investigation department of any force in the country.

". . . though," Mr. Chestley immediately added a rider, "no doubt a comfort to the member of the medical profession concerned."

"Dr. Paston," said Sloan again.

"But irrelevant." The coroner would not be gainsaid.

"Really, sir?"

"Post-mortems," declared the coroner, "do not always confirm the certified cause of death."

Sloan could well believe this. People could be ill with one thing and die from another. Easily. And doctors could be wrong. Even more easily.

"Mind you," said the coroner, unexpectedly reverting to his own profession, "counsel's opinion isn't always perfect either."

Sloan cleared his throat and made a valiant attempt to get back to the business in hand. "The superintendent says . . ."

"But the system's better than it was."

Sloan said he was glad to hear it.

"Not so simple, though."

"Nothing," said Sloan with unfeigned heartiness, "is as simple as it used to be."

The coroner adjusted his pince-nez again. "Before they had Dabbe and his fancy scientific outfit . . ."

"Yes?"

"They used to have a couple of old women."

"Did they, sir?" Sloan shifted his weight from one leg to the other. He hadn't come here on a busy day to be lectured on ancient customs. He was a police officer and he'd come about a sudden death.

"They called them searchers."

"Really, sir?" It was Sloan's invariable practise to allow other people to give him information—however recondite—without let or hindrance. Or interruption.

"Two of them," said the coroner gratuitously, "used to totter along to the graveside and view the dead before burial."

"Did they, sir?" He himself felt no necessity to bring the Bow Street runners into the conversation.

"They made up their minds what the cause of death was."

"It was one way of doing it, sir, I suppose."

"None of this stainless-steel nonsense," said the coroner, dismissing several thousand pounds' worth of highly sophisticated forensic pathology equipment with the wave of a hand.

"No." That would have saved the taxpayers a packet, though Sloan did not say so.

"Then they'd pop round and tell the parish clerk."

"No red tape," observed Sloan, aware that some remark was expected of him.

"He kept a stroke record," said the coroner.

"Saved a lot of paper work," agreed Sloan, entering into the spirit of the thing in spite of himself.

"And before you could say 'Jack Robinson,'" said the coroner, "you had your bill of mortality."

"Not," remarked Sloan, "quite as accurate as the registrar general's statistics but good enough."

The coroner readjusted his pince-nez and looked thoughtful. "No three-ring civil servant circus either, of course."

"And so," said Sloan, making a game attempt to get back to the matter in hand, "you'll just notify the registrar general that Miss Wansdyke died from the complications of diabetes?"

"I shall say," said the coroner cautiously, "that the

pathologist so advises me and that I deem an inquest
not necessary in all the circumstances that have been
presented to me. I may, of course," he added uncon-
vincingly, "be in error."

* * *

Mr. Chestley might have considered this last possibility a little more seriously had he been present when
Sloan got back to the police station.

Detective Constable Crosby rang in just after he
reached his desk.

"You've done what, Crosby?" demanded Sloan martially. "Say that again!"

"Found her dog, sir."

"You're sure it's hers?"

"Long legs and short hair, sir, like you and Dr.
Dabbe said. An Airedale."

"Answering to the name of Isolde?" said Sloan. It
was not a name he for one would care to go around the
streets of Berebury late at night calling out aloud, but
even so . . .

"Not answering to any name, sir. Not now."

"What do you mean?"

"Dead," said Crosby lugubriously.

Chapter 6

No one can stop until there's nothing left.

At the Berebury District General Hospital, Nurse Briony Petforth came off duty from Fleming Ward with relief. She thankfully changed out of her uniform into a soft blue and brown mixture matching skirt and jerkin that went well with her auburn hair. After a moment or two's consideration she selected a rather more dressy blouse to go under her jerkin and slipped a couple of strings of contrasting beads into her handbag. They would do for later.

She debated with herself for a moment whether she should telephone the ante-natal clinic again but in the end she decided against it. Roger Elspin knew where she was going. He would come along as soon as he could get away from the clinic and the ward. She sighed. Obstetrics was no speciality for a clock watcher.

Dermatology, she decided, was what he could take up after they got married. Skin patients never needed their doctor urgently in the middle of a dinner party, or got him up in the small hours of the night either. They never died—and seldom got better for that matter— and yet were always profoundly grateful for whatever could be done for them that helped. Dermatology it would have to be.

Having thus mentally resolved the professional fate of one promising young obstetric surgeon, she slipped on a duffle coat and made her way across the town to North Berebury. Her cousin George Wansdyke and his wife, Pauline, lived in a detached house in Cullum Crescent. They received her with relief.

"Poor Briony," said Pauline Wansdyke with a shudder. "Come in and sit down. I couldn't have looked at Aunt Beatrice like you did. I really couldn't."

"I didn't mind." Briony brushed this to one side, marvelling, as she always did, at Pauline's capacity for striking just the wrong note.

"I couldn't have done it," repeated Pauline Wansdyke dramatically, "not if I'd been the last person on earth."

"We've all got to die," said Briony briefly. "There's nothing unnatural about that."

"That's the trouble with doctors and nurses," complained Pauline Wansdyke. "They get so unfeeling."

"No, they don't," countered Briony spiritedly.

"Dr. Paston wasn't in the least bit sympathetic about my bad back," said Mrs. Wansdyke, not listening. "Just rheumatism, he said, and nobody knew how painful it was."

"Doctors and nurses have feelings just like everyone else," insisted Briony Petforth, forbearing to remind her that everyone—but everyone—had known all about how painful Pauline's back had been. "More than some people, actually."

"Not Dr. Paston," said Pauline, always inclined to the personal. "He was quite unfeeling, I can assure you."

"But . . ."

"He gave me some white tablets that didn't begin to touch the pain and told me to go away."

"He did say to come back if you weren't any better though," put in her husband fairly.

"It's just," continued Briony Petforth more to herself than to the Wansdykes, "that doctors and nurses have to adjust to all the unhappiness around them all the time early on."

"Learn to live with it." George Wansdyke nodded.

"But I don't see why . . ." began Pauline.

"Otherwise," said Briony, between clenched teeth, "they'd go stark, raving mad, that's why!"

"Pauline was just going to make some tea," interposed George Wansdyke swiftly. He was adept now at smoothing over any hiatus created by his wife's ap-

proach to the world. "And the children are in bed, so
sit down and tell me exactly what happened at the hospital."

Briony sank thankfully into a chair. "Nothing much,
really, George. I identified Aunt Beatrice as Beatrice
Gwendoline Wansdyke, that's all."

"Sorry I wasn't there," he said. "I would have
come."

"I know you would," she said. "Couldn't be helped."

"I've been on to Mortons'," he said carefully. "They
don't know what all the fuss was about either."

She shrugged her shoulders. "No harm done. In fact
now we know for sure that it was the diabetes, don't
we?"

"Yes, indeed," agreed George. "Not that there was
ever any doubt in my mind."

"There was in someone's," pointed out Briony, "otherwise . . ."

"Quite," said George Wansdyke. "Anyway, everything should be plain sailing from now on, shouldn't
it?"

"I hope so," said the girl fervently. "I hope so."

There was a pause and then she said more casually,
"Roger's coming round to collect me as soon as he
comes off duty."

Wansdyke nodded. "Right."

"We're going out somewhere to eat." She pushed
back a stray lock of hair. "Not that I'm hungry."

"No," said Wansdyke, "but I daresay you'll have
plans to make."

She looked at him curiously. "Perhaps."

"If you're not going to live in the house in Ridley
Road you'll have to decide what to do about it pretty
quickly, my dear. An empty house is just an open invi-
tation to squatters these days. You can't just leave it."

"Don't rush me, George. Not yet. I'm . . . I'm not
used to Aunt Beatrice not being there yet."

"Sorry. Take all the time you need, Briony." He
pointed to a bureau in the corner. "I haven't really begun to look at her affairs anyway. I've been devilish
busy at work. Malcolm's been on this export trip to the
States. He'll be back on Thursday though for this prod-

uct launching we've got laid on and then I'll be more my own man again, thank goodness."

Briony yawned. "Poor Aunt Beatrice never found her particular crock of gold at the end of the rainbow, did she?"

George Wansdyke shook his head. "Not that I know of. But she enjoyed looking for it."

"Perhaps that's all that matters."

"Travelling hopefully, you mean?" He gave her a quizzical look.

Briony wasn't really listening. "That's your front doorbell, isn't it? Roger's got away early if it's him."

It wasn't Dr. Roger Elspin at the front door. It was Detective Inspector Sloan and Detective Constable Crosby.

The superintendent never gave up. Bulldogs as a breed had nothing on Superintendent Leeyes when his jaws were locked firmly onto a problem. Nor was he one to accept a dead end. Immediately after writing off the post-mortem he had proceeded to turn his mind to other aspects of the death of Miss Beatrice Wansdyke.

It was therefore not very long before he came up with the question which came—like Death—late or soon to Everyman—or at any rate to every policeman.

"Who benefits, Sloan?" he demanded to know. "Tell me that."

Which was how it was that Dectective Inspector Sloan and Detective Constable Crosby came to be ringing the doorbell of a house called "The Laurels" in Cullum Crescent, Berebury, at this particular moment. George Wansdyke admitted them.

"Of course. Come in," he said, when Sloan had explained who they were. "We were expecting someone to come along to tell us what all the fuss was about."

Sloan decided that that line would serve as as good an introduction as he was ever likely to get.

"We're sorry to have bothered you, sir," he said, slipping easily into a semideferential manner, which, had they been privileged to witness it, would have at the same time both considerably startled Larky Nolson and vastly amused Mrs. Margaret Sloan. It was nicely done.

The tone implied apology without actually meaning it. "Some sort of mix-up somewhere along the line . . ."

"No trouble," said Wansdyke, equally magnanimous. "Briony . . . Inspector, this is my cousin, Miss Petforth."

"We have met," said Sloan. "At the hospital."

"Oh, really?" He looked up as his wife came back into the room. "Pauline, dear, these are police officers who have come to tell us about poor Aunt Beatrice."

"Poor Aunt Beatrice," echoed Pauline Wansdyke without noticeable conviction.

"Briony—Miss Petforth, here—stood in for me at the identification," said George to Sloan.

"You're her executor, though, sir, aren't you?"

"I am indeed." He shrugged his shoulders ruefully. "Not that I imagine that the duties are likely to be—er—exactly onerous."

"Oh?" said Sloan, utterly deadpan.

"Her pension rights die with her, of course, as she didn't reach sixty. . . ."

Like the mustard left on the plate, that was where the pension fund money was, thought Sloan to himself.

". . . and the house goes outright to Briony here," continued George.

Briony flushed but said nothing.

"I see," said Sloan mendaciously. "And the residue?"

"She wasn't a rich woman," said George Wansdyke.

"No?"

"My grandparents left her a little, naturally, including a small stake in the firm."

Sloan looked expectant. "She wasn't their only child though?"

"Of course not." George Wansdyke looked distinctly uncomfortable. "Otherwise she wouldn't have a niece, would she? But she had nursed them both, and my father—her brother—had built up the firm into something by then."

Sloan, who could count as well as the next man, said, "And Miss Petforth's mother?"

"Cut off with a shilling," said Briony, flushing again.

"She was not mentioned in the wills of either of my grandparents," said Wansdyke.

"I see."

"My mother, you might as well know, ran off with a no-good-boyo," said Briony Petforth, showing a working acquaintance with the works of the late Dylan Thomas as well as a sense of humour.

"My grandparents were very old-fashioned," said Wansdyke stiffly.

"When my great aunt married the coachman," said Pauline Wansdyke, "her parents went into black and never mentioned her name again. They were Hartley-Powells, of course."

"They turned my Auntie Nellie's picture to the wall," contributed Detective Constable Crosby chattily.

Everyone looked in his direction.

"She didn't marry anyone," said Crosby. "That was the trouble."

Pauline Wansdyke wasn't used to being upstaged.

"They drew the window blinds, too, on the day she married," she said firmly, "as if she'd died, and then they rubbed her name out of the family Bible."

"My parents did die, Inspector," said Briony softly. "In a car accident when we were little."

"We?" queried Sloan.

The interrogative hung unacknowledged for a moment.

"My brother and I," said Briony after a pause.

"Winding up Beatrice's estate," interposed George Wansdyke fussily, "won't be a difficult matter."

"Good," said Sloan warmly. If George Wansdyke believed that, then like somebody else, he could believe anything.

"She had a friend called Hilda Collins," said Wansdyke obliquely. "She gets a little. An eighth, actually. So does Dr. Paston."

"Her general practitioner?"

"He was an old friend as well as her doctor, Inspector. He'd been very good to her over the years over this chronic complaint of hers."

"Diabetes," said Briony Petforth rather crossly. "Why doesn't everyone say so and call it what it was?"

"Quite so," said Sloan. "And?"

"My children get a small sum between them," continued Wansdyke. "In trust, naturally, seeing that they're underage."

"Naturally," concurred Sloan. Trust laws might seem a contradiction in terms but they knew all about untrustworthy trustees down at the police station. The mediaevalists had done better still. They used to put the just judges on one side of a painting and the unjust ones on the other.

"It won't amount to much, of course," said Wansdyke. "Another eighth."

"Of course," echoed Sloan, reserving judgement on this.

"Briony gets the same as well as the house."

Detective Inspector Sloan did some mental arithmetic out loud. "Four eighths make a half, sir, don't they?"

"They do," said George Wansdyke reluctantly.

"That leaves a half," said Sloan.

Wansdyke coughed. "That goes to Briony's brother, Nicholas." He spread his hands open and apart in an age-old gesture. "If we can find him, that is."

Briony Petforth looked up. "The dog's missing too."

* * *

However Dickensian an impression the coroner's office gave to the casual visitor, it still sported a telephone. Mrs. Chestley's personal secretary was middle-aged and competent. The calls she allowed to be put through to her employer were only those she knew he would want to take. To all other callers he was either "engaged with a client" or "in court."

"Mr. Chestley," she said now, "I have Dr. John Paston on the line."

"Put him through," he said immediately—as she had known he would. There was a pause. Then: "John . . ."

"That you, Chestley? Paston here. What's all this about my death certificate for Beatrice Wansdyke?"

"No problem," said the coroner.

"I've had the relatives round my neck and I can't get hold of Dabbe."

"No problem," repeated the coroner. "Your friend

and medical colleague, the pathologist, says she died of diabetes, too."

"That's a relief," said Paston frankly. "For a moment I thought . . ."

"Doctors have been known to differ," said the solicitor mildly. "Especially after death."

"I was afraid I might have missed something," said the general practitioner. "I'm not as young as I used to be and I've got a lot on my mind."

"If you have missed anything," the coroner said drily, "it wasn't anything that the pathologist could find."

"Shouldn't have wanted to slip up with her. The nephew's wife is a first-class menace. Besides, Beatrice was a decent sort."

Both men, professional realists, knew that the latter was very much a secondary consideration compared with the former.

"Of course," said Chestley, "Dabbe did a lot of hedging about in case anything shows up in his tissue testing."

"Pathologists," said the general practitioner, "are getting as bad as solicitors at that these days."

"Nothing's as certain as it used to be," countered Robert Chestley profoundly. "The law has always known it. Medicine's just catching on."

"The patient doesn't like his physician to share his uncertainty with him," responded Paston. "I've tried it and I know."

"Dabbe does let you have a copy of his report, doesn't he?"

"He does but I daresay it won't surprise me now. She was getting all sorts of signs and symptoms that indicated she needed more insulin. I saw her twice last week and told her to step up her dose each time."

"Ah."

"I should have thought it would have done the trick myself—surprising it didn't really—but you never can tell."

"No."

"And of course she lived alone. Then if you do go

over the edge of safety there's no one there to haul you back."

"She might not have acted upon your advice," pointed out the coroner, always able to find something to cavil at, and well used to doctors who wondered if they should have done more.

"I'll have you know, Chestley, that patients are usually more obedient than clients."

"Just as well," riposted the man of law neatly. "Clients who don't take our advice bring in a, lot of work. Yours only die."

This response set up quite a different train of thought in the general practitioner. His tone changed completely. "Bob, I'm sending my junior partner round to see you."

"Peter McCavity?"

"I've persuaded him to consult you at last. Took a bit of doing."

"I can believe that."

"He's—er—got himself into a—er—little difficulty."

"Again?"

"Yes." The doctor sighed. "Yes. Again."

"The old problem?"

There was a pause. "I'm very much afraid so."

* * *

"The dog it was that died, eh, Sloan?" said the superintendent thoughtfully when the detective inspector got back to the police station.

"So Constable Crosby says, sir." Sloan toyed with the note he had made.

"And how did he find out?"

"Poking about in Ridley Road," said Sloan, looking out of the window.

"Poking about?"

"Digging," supplied Sloan uncomfortably.

"Where?"

"Miss Wansdyke's garden."

"He'll be the death of me, that boy, one day," breathed Leeyes.

"Of us all," said Sloan feelingly.

"Not so much as 'by your leave'?"

"No."

"Anyone's permission?"

"No."

"Search warrant?"

"Wouldn't know what that looked like, I daresay."

"Just went along with his spade?"

"Shouldn't be surprised."

"And his bucket," said Leeyes, "like he was at the seaside?"

"Probably."

"What will the neighbours say?"

Taking this literally, Sloan flipped his note over. "One of them gave him a cup of tea—a Mrs. Stroude. She confirms that Miss Wansdyke spent the whole of Friday evening looking for the dog. She heard her whistling and calling until quite late. And she saw her out and about early Saturday morning ditto."

"By which time the dog was dead and buried?"

"Presumably."

"Where?"

"Not far from a small compost heap at the bottom of the garden."

"Crosby knew where to look?" Leeyes sounded disbelieving.

Sloan cleared his throat and said carefully, "He tells me that in one of his training courses they had a lesson on how to identify disturbed ground."

"With pictures, I suppose," grunted Leeyes. "When I was a constable we were supposed to work that sort of thing out for ourselves."

"Yes, sir." Disturbed ground always meant something, all the same. The archaeologists knew that.

"Julius Caesar was here," said the superintendent, "and all that."

"Yes, sir."

"So he knew what to look for?"

"He found the dog," said Sloan elliptically.

"The dead don't bury the dead," said the superintendent.

"No." Sloan acknowledged this immediately. "From what he says there seems little doubt that someone . . ."

"Person or persons unknown . . ." intervened Leeyes.

"Er—quite, sir—buried the dog just after dark on Friday evening."

"How do we know that?"

"I gather Mrs. Stroude is the sort of neighbour who would have noticed—er—unusual activity in the next-door garden in daylight."

"I don't know where we'd get without inquisitive neighbours," said Leeyes frankly. "I reckon that's what keeps people on the straight and narrow—not morality at all."

"This one is positive nothing sinister went on in the garden in the early afternoon," said Sloan. He paused. "She went out a little later on though. That's when she noticed the car."

"What car?"

"A blue Allegro," said Sloan carefully. He paused. "A very battered one."

"Did she know it?" He grunted. "Women don't usually."

"Oh, yes."

"Do we know it?" enquired Leeyes heavily.

"Yes."

"Not the battered blue Allegro that we all know?"

"Dr. McCavity's," said Sloan, "from the sound of it."

"Hrrrrrmph," said Leeyes.

"Yes, sir," said Sloan. "Quite."

"How," enquired Leeyes pertinently, "did the dog get from house to garden?"

"How it got out of the house is what bothered Miss Wansdyke. She didn't know about it being dead in the garden, of course. She'd left it locked indoors when she went to school as usual. She was so upset about that fact that she told Mrs. Stroude she was putting the chain on her door that night."

"So someone opens the door with a key . . ." He paused. "Or do you think our promising young Sherlock Holmes was so busy digging up the dog that he wouldn't have noticed a break-in?"

"Miss Wansdyke would have done," said Sloan realistically.

Leeyes nodded. "Right. Then the door gets opened with a key, and someone kills Fido."

"Isolde," said Sloan distantly.

"You having me on, Sloan?" growled Leeyes.

"No, sir."

There was a pause, then: "I had forgotten we were in a superior part of the town."

"Quite, sir."

"Sloan . . ."

"Sir?"

"There's an old saying about dogs."

"Letting sleeping ones lie?" ventured Sloan.

"No," roared Leeyes. "Certainly not. We're police officers, man, not politicians."

"Sorry, sir." He coughed. "Another old saying, I think you said. . . ."

"Love me, love my dog," said Leeyes.

"Yes, sir. Of course, sir, but . . ."

"Have we got a case of 'Hate me, hate my dog' on our hands, Sloan? Tell me that. . . ."

"I hope not, sir."

"Sloan"—Leeyes had a second thought—"how do we know that Miss Wansdyke didn't find the dog dead herself later on the Saturday or Sunday and see that it was decently buried in her garden?"

"Because it had had its throat cut," said Sloan chillingly.

Chapter 7

Ah, no, let be! For the Philosopher's Stone,
Called the Elixir, never can be known.

Just as, in the immortal words of the poet, even the
weariest river winds somewhere safe to the sea, so eventually every tired policeman finds his way at last to his
own fireside. Lightly brushing a kiss onto his wife's
cheeks, Detective Inspector Sloan dropped thankfully
into an armchair.

"You'll miss me when I'm in the hospital," said Margaret Sloan. "When I'm not here to come home to . . ."

He did not attempt to answer this. "I'll know all
about it, though, when you get back, won't I?" he insisted in mock despair. "A baby crying . . . nappies
everywhere . . . another mouth to feed . . ."

"Talking of food . . ." she said, disappearing hastily
in the direction of the kitchen.

When she came back he told her about the dog.

"Poor thing," she said, distressed. "Whoever would
want to do a thing like that?"

"I don't know." He stuffed a cushion behind his head
and said what was uppermost in his mind. "It's not a lot
to go on—a dead dog."

"And a quarter of a million pounds," she reminded
him.

"The family are all carrying on as if she's only left
twopence ha'penny," said Sloan.

"Perhaps they really don't know."

"For my money," said Sloan with a fine disregard for
metaphor, "someone somewhere does."

"And she did die naturally," said Margaret Sloan.

"The dog didn't," said her husband obliquely.

She shuddered a little. "Whose money will it be then?"

"You're as bad as the superintendent." Sloan stretched his legs out in front of the fire. "He keeps on asking that, too, only he doesn't put it quite so nicely."

"Gain usually comes into evil somewhere, doesn't it?" she said.

"Yes, my love." He was quite willing to go along with that: in fact he didn't know of any policeman who wouldn't be. If gain didn't come into evil then what you had instead wasn't crime at all but a suitable case for treatment—medical treatment.

"Immediate gain, that is," she said seriously, sitting down, too, by the fire. She stared into the flames for a moment and then said, "There's something sinister in one of the nursery rhymes about growing rich, isn't there?"

"Been doing your homework, have you?" he teased her, casting about in his mind for the allusion. "Ready for you-know-who?"

She smiled wanly and quoted, " 'When I grow rich . . . say the bells of Shoreditch.' "

" 'The bells of London Town,' " he said. Nursery rhymes were uncannily prescient. Then something stirred in his own childhood memory. "The Old Bailey comes into that, too, doesn't it?"

" 'When will you pay me?' " she sang softly.

" 'Say the bells at Old Bailey.' " He completed the couplet in a lower register.

"Trust a copper to remember that bit," she said, her turn to tease.

"Plenty of debts to society have been paid at the Old Bailey in its time."

"We shouldn't be joking about all this, should we?" she said quickly. "Not with Miss Wansdyke and her dog both lying dead . . ."

Somewhere in one of the books they had had handed out to them at the ante-natal clinic had been some advice about how a couple should comfort themselves during the wife's pregnancy. They shouldn't move house, for instance, or indulge in great arguments. Whims, however bizarre, should be indulged. Strange fancies for out-of-season strawberries or fresh oysters should be pandered to. Layettes should be prepared but—and the good books stressed this—pregnancy was no time for philosophical doubts. The profundities of life should be allowed to take second place to the most profound experience of all living.

He gave a huge yawn and deliberately steered the conversation towards more neutral ground. "There's one funny thing, though, Margaret. . . ."

"What's that?"

"The family have gone all quiet about the main ben-eficiary, Nicholas Petforth, Briony's brother. They say they don't know where he is."

"Perhaps," she said consideringly, "he'll come home again now that there's something to come back for."

"There! What did I say?" He gave her an affection-ate grin. "You're really as bad as the superintendent after all. . . ."

"Me?" she said indignantly.

"All he does is concentrate on who gains." He stretched his legs out before the blaze in the hearth. "At least it means that I know what tomorrow's first job is going to be."

She looked up. "What's that?"

"Find Master Petforth."

"Not," she enquired ironically, "a search and destroy mission—destroy with great wealth, I mean."

"No." He shook his head. "We'll just put the word out. That's all."

His wife stared dreamily into the fire and quoted:

> " 'Instantly the under-
>   standing Seraphim
> Laid their fingers on their lips
> And went to look for him.' "

"Jane Austen?" he hazarded. If they had a daughter she was going to have "Jane" among her given names. Margaret went on:

" 'Stole across the Zodiac,
    Harnessed Charles's Wain,
    And whispered round the Nebulae . . .' "

He relaxed. "Nothing like that. Don't worry. Just a
few questions here and there. If he's in Calleshire," said
Sloan confidently, "we'll pick him up tomorrow. If we
have to ask questions outside the county of course it'll
take longer. . . . What is it?" His whole tone changed
suddenly as he saw a spasm of pain crossing her face.
"Margaret . . . Margaret, what is it? What's wrong?
Is it . . ."

"I've just thought . . . that horrible nursery
rhyme."

"Oranges and lemons?"

She stared at him. "I've remembered how it fin-
ishes."

"Don't look like that, my love," he pleaded. "You
frightened me. For a moment I thought . . ."

" 'Here comes a candle to light you to bed,' " she
intoned, " 'and here comes a chopper to chop off your
head.' "

*   *   *

It wasn't the Seraphim who found out where Nicholas Petforth was in the end. Or, at least, not directly.

It was Detective Constable William Edward Crosby.

People who went native these days usually did so in
one of two ways. They either took to the road or they
joined a commune.

Putting the word out in the county had had the de-
sired effect.

They learned down at the Berebury Police Station
fairly early on that their man wasn't on the road in Calleshire. He was too young for that game for a start and
those who were walking the countryside—that pathetic
group whose worldly possessions were clutched to them,
who tramped from somewhere to anywhere like a variety of land-locked Flying Dutchmen, without either an-
chor or rudder, answering to any wind or to no wind at

all—had not come across anyone sounding like Miss Beatrice Wansdyke's nephew. There were fewer of such travellers about these days, but those that there were were conspicuous and—uphill and down dale—they obligingly stopped long enough to tell the police that Nicholas Petforth wasn't one of their number. Mind you, stopping wasn't something they liked to do. If you stopped, you had to think: and for them thinking was the only unbearable activity.

Today's drop-outs didn't walk the countryside. When they wanted to cast off society's links they squatted: especially the younger ones. If enough of them squatted together somehow the community became a commune.

It had fallen to Detective Constable Crosby's lot to call on the one in the town of Luston.

"You can't miss it, lad," the friendly station sergeant at Luston had told him, adding, "I daresay there'll be a bite left to eat in our canteen when you get back." He chuckled. "If you still feel like eating, that is."

Any connection between what went on in this Calleshire commune and the dreams and the reality of the days of the French Commune of an earlier age must have been purely coincidental. Urban decay had reached the old centre of the industrial town: urban renewal hadn't. Constable Crosby made his way to a faded early nineteenth-century town house that in its prime had had some considerable style to it. Now its paintwork was peeling and some of its windows were boarded up. Other windows sported blankets doing duty as curtains. Somehow, though, the once-graceful building had contrived to retain an air of decayed gentility—distinction, even.

Detective Constable Crosby's pounding on the front door shook it visibly but produced no answer from within. Immediately, however, the door of the house next door flew open and a raven-haired woman put her head out.

"If you're the gas," she said, "you're wasting your time. It's cut off."

Crosby said he wasn't the gas.

"They've found a way round the electricity meter for sure," she said.

Crosby said he could well believe it.

"And if you're the Water Board," she grimaced, completing a trinity of public supply undertakings, "you needn't worry. They don't use it." She rolled her eyes. "The whole place stinks."

By now Crosby had been able to appreciate this fact for himself. Château Commune certainly had a bouquet all its own.

"I can tell you one thing for sure," she cackled. "They can't read bills in there."

"Some people have all the luck," said Crosby.

The neighbour's head, which seemed as disembodied behind its owner's front door as the Cheshire cat's on its wall, looked him up and down.

"Come to serve a summons, 'ave you?" she asked shrewdly.

In a way it was a tribute to his manner, if not his suit.

"I'm making enquiries," responded Crosby.

"You'll be lucky." She sniffed. She jerked her head towards the other house. "Not many of them get up in the mornings, I can tell you."

He looked up at the blind windows.

"Work's a dirty word with that lot," she said.

"Some of them must do some," protested the young policeman in spite of himself. They'd been very firm in his primary school about tying the male image to the work ethic. The boys hadn't learned knitting. They'd been taught instead that men must work. The corollary that women must weep ("Georgie Porgy kissed the girls and made them cry") they'd been left to find out for themselves in the playground afterwards. "You can't live without working," he said, though you couldn't be a policeman long without meeting a group who tried to do just that.

"Two or three of the fellers do go out to work," she conceded. "None of the girls." She raised her eyebrows heavenwards. "What they do all day long don't bear thinking about."

It was quite apparent though from her keen expression that she thought about it a lot.

Crosby kept silent.

She jerked her head towards the next-door building. "Beats me," she said, sucking her teeth, "how the police let them get away with squatting."

Crosby drew breath. "Civil law . . ."

"Take Fred Smith's boy down the road."

"Well?"

"They had him for breaking and entering last week."

"Did they?"

"Camera shop in Calleford High Street."

"Ah."

"Don't you go and say that that's different."

"I shan't."

"This lot next door," she said richly, "did their breaking and entering and they stayed."

"I can see that."

"And nobody's touched them for anything."

"No." It was funny how the word "touched" hung about the law.

"It's not right."

"No, madam." If anything, squatting offended the police even more than it did the public. "But the law is that . . ."

"You looking for anyone in particular?" she interrupted him off-handedly.

"Tall, youngish lad," said Crosby, also cutting the cackle and getting to the horses. "Auburn hair. Still a bit freckled."

"There's one or two of 'em in there," she said slyly, "that shouldn't be."

"I daresay. This chap . . ."

She jerked her head. "And not what you'd expect, either."

"Oh?"

"A couple of clever dicks and some girls who should know better."

"From good homes, you mean?" he said naïvely.

Her face assumed a curious expression.

"If that's what you'd call Calle Castle . . ."

"The duke's daughter?" Crosby took another look up at the dilapidated house.

"His youngest." She sniffed.

"Bit of a change, wasn't it?"

"I should think they had their hands full with her at home. She's a one, all right. Oh, her father came round and made noises."

"I'll bet."

"It didn't do any good. It was her mother that got her out."

"How?" asked Crosby in spite of himself.

"Sent the chauffeur round each week with a box of groceries and a brace of pheasants."

"How did that do it?"

The face grinned at his innocence. "The Lady Alicia was all for sending them back, snooty-like, unopened."

"Fair enough."

"Said it made her feel different."

"I'll bet it did," said Crosby warmly.

"But the others wouldn't let her," cackled the woman shrewishly. "They ate 'em."

"Too bad. Then she grew up or something?"

"After a bit," she crowed, "she got to see the others were making a fool of her."

"Sponging," pronounced Crosby.

"Enjoying what they said they despised," mimicked the woman in high lady-like tones. She grinned. "Give her another ten years and she'll be opening flower shows with the best of them."

"This fellow that I'm looking for . . ."

"Called Nick?" hazarded the woman.

"Could be."

"You're wasting your time."

"Not here?"

"One of the workers. Goes off early."

"Where?"

"Up the motorway site."

"Thanks." Crosby turned to go. Then he stopped. "You'd miss them now, wouldn't you?" he said.

She slammed the door.

* * *

"The bank," reported Sloan gloomily, "will surrender details of their late client's account if . . ."

"Yes?" said Superintendent Leeyes eagerly, leaning forward across his desk.

"If," repeated Sloan, "we get a court order."

"Bah!" said Leeyes, who never in any circumstances whatsoever himself divulged confidential police information to any unauthorised person or institution.

"And not without one," underlined Sloan.

"Obstructionists . . ."

"Any other assistance that we may require," repeated Sloan fluently, "they will, of course, be only too happy to give us."

"The source of the money," said Leeyes promptly.

"I asked them that," said Sloan.

"Well?"

"They said, 'What money?' as bland as butter."

"What about her life-style?" said Leeyes in a challenging fashion. "That didn't go with a quarter of a million pounds, did it?"

"That," admitted Sloan, "did seem to strike a chord with the bank manager."

"Well," said Leeyes tartly, "she wasn't exactly living it up, was she?"

"It's not," ventured Sloan cautiously, "quite the same down there at the bank as it is round here moneywise."

"I should hope not," retorted Leeyes speedily. There was a pause. Then he said, "Just exactly what are you getting at, Sloan?"

"Down there, sir, they're more used than we are here to folks without money spending it."

"Drinking whisky on a beer income," said Leeyes graphically.

"And to customers with it not spending it," added Sloan fairly.

"Orange juice on a brandy income."

"I understand," replied Sloan drily, "that they've got a fair number of those too."

Shaking his head at what he saw as a waste of natural resources, Leeyes said, "Anything else?"

"Every time I came up with a question they referred me to their client's executor."

"Bertram George Wansdyke," said the superintendent, who always did his homework.

"He doesn't use the Bertram," Sloan informed him. "They told me that at the bank."

"Don't blame him."

"He's always known as George."

"Never Bertram," noted Leeyes. "People can be funny about Christian names."

"Watch out for any man who calls his son Samson," said Sloan.

"You and your wife got all that sort of thing lined up all right, Sloan?" asked Leeyes gruffly.

"What? Oh, yes, sir. Thank you, sir." Potential names of babies were not in short supply in the Sloan ménage. On the contrary. And had they been, Sloan's mother had a reserve supply.

"Mind you," said the superintendent reminiscently, "our brigadier was called Cecil so it doesn't always signify."

"I was once attacked by a social misfit called Algernon," contributed Sloan. The superintendent had to be diverted from recounting his wartime experiences at all costs or the day was lost. "At least, his mother called him Algernon and the judge called him a social misfit and I . . ."

"This Bertram George Wansdyke . . ."

"A partner in Wansdyke and Darnley."

"The firm down by the bridge?"

"Them. Plastics manufacturers."

"Anything," enquired Leeyes, rolling his eyes, "to do with the celebrated Malcolm Darnley?"

"Everything."

"Good God! The agitator?"

"Conservationist," murmured Sloan mildly, "is what he calls himself."

"He's practically maniacal about it."

" 'Dedicated,' " said Sloan austerely, "is the word the newspapers use."

"Inspector Harpe can't get a roadway corner in the whole of Calleshire straightened," declared Leeyes. "Every time he wants a tree down it turns out to have a preservation order clapped on it."

"That's Malcolm Darnley," agreed Sloan. "He insists

that trees do not get up and hit passing motorists. He wins every time."

"And the Town Council can't widen the roads round by the cattle market either. Every building they want out of the way turns out to have had Queen Elizabeth sleeping in it or something."

"Listed," said Sloan more technically.

"And I have to have two good men and true down there every market day when they should be catching villains."

" 'His mission in life,' " Sloan quoted something he'd read in the local newspaper, " 'is the preservation of the environment.' "

"The man's a first-class nuisance."

"Public-spirited," murmured Sloan, "is the name of the game."

"Hrrrrrmph."

"Anyway, George Wansdyke seems able to cope."

"Firm all right"

"Appears to be flourishing," said Sloan. "They turn out the more rarefied plastic parts for industry and medicine and so forth. They do a lot of the research and development, too, I'm told. Take on promising young science graduates and all that sort of thing."

"No word of any money troubles?"

"None." He coughed. "Anyway, George Wansdyke doesn't get anything himself from his aunt's estate. His children get an eighth between them in trust, that's all."

"George Wansdyke," pronounced Superintendent Leeyes didactically, "is the sole executor of an estate that everyone believes to be small. . . ."

They were interrupted by the telephone.

"Who?" said Leeyes testily. "Well, put him through, of course." He looked at Sloan. "It's Dr. Dabbe." His tone changed. "Good morning, Doctor. About Beatrice Gwendoline Wansdyke . . . Yes . . . Yes, yes . . . I know all the background . . . Yes . . . Diabetes . . . Insulin . . . What's that?" His eyebrows disappeared upwards. "What did you say? . . . Yes, I've got that. . . . Insulin . . . No insulin? Do you mind repeating that? Yes, that's what I thought you said. I'll send a man round for the report straightaway. . . . Thank you." He made to put the telephone receiver down, then changed his mind. "Doctor, are you still there? . . . Look here, how are you on dogs? . . . What? . . . No, not betting on them . . . doing post-mortems on them. . . . On one, actually . . . We may want one done . . . That's very kind of you . . . Thank you." He did put the telephone down this time. And then he turned back to Sloan, his face a study. "The pathologist reports that there was no trace of insulin in Beatrice Wansdyke's blood. He reckons she's been without it for several days."

Chapter 8

My face is wan and wears a leaden look;
If you try science you'll be brought to book.

The foreman on the motorway construction site was a much-tried man. He had, however, long ago reached that stage of controlled despair when he regarded each fresh burden with a certain masochistic satisfaction as providing further evidence of a malign fate's continued unkindness to him.

"Police?" he said to Detective Constable Crosby, rolling his eyes. "What is it this time? Something fallen off the back of a lorry again?"

"Not today," said Crosby cautiously. "So far."

"Or have you come to tell me that you've found that load of aggregate that got nicked on the Calleford Road?"

"Not yet," said Crosby, "but I daresay we shall."

"That's all very fine and large," said the foreman, "but it won't help me. I had to get onto the quarry sharp for another load."

"Perhaps next time," suggested the constable, "the driver will use another transport café."

The foreman gave him a shrewd look. "Mother Meg's again? I've always said it was a proper thieves' kitchen."

"Meals come a bit expensive there sometimes." Detective Constable Crosby surveyed the motorway site from the vantage point beside the foreman's hut. "Mucking Calleshire about a bit, aren't you?"

"Don't you start. . . ."

"Like being on the moon but dirtier."

The foreman twisted his lips. "You should have heard them at the enquiry."

Crosby grinned. "Our Mr. Malcolm Darnley from Berebury there?"

"It's a wonder he didn't get arrested."

"It's a free country."

"Stabbed in the back then," said the foreman.

The constable waved an arm. "Well, he did have something to complain about, didn't he?"

"Said he'd lie down under the first bulldozer."

"Someone nick that too?"

"Wish he had and all," grumbled the foreman.

"Saved a lot of trouble, would it?" said the constable, looking 'round.

"Someone," said the foreman with deep conviction, "will put that man Darnley in a wooden overcoat one day."

"A cement one, more likely," said Crosby, looking around at the desolate waste of concrete that surrounded them.

"What? Oh, yes. I daresay."

"It's been done before," said the constable seriously. "At least we think it's been done before. It's not easy to prove."

"I can see," said the foreman, casting his eyes in the general direction of an embryo fly-over, "that you'd likely be a bit short on evidence."

Detective Constable Crosby followed his gaze. "No more bother with that crane over there?" he enquired solicitously.

"Not that I've heard about." The foreman rolled his eyes. "Not that I get to hear everything, mind you."

"No," said Crosby consideringly, "you wouldn't, would you?"

"Not in my job," agreed the foreman. "Mark you, there's some things I don't want to know about, thank you very much."

"I can see that," said the constable.

The foreman indicated the crane. "We lock it up of nights now."

"Good," said Crosby pleasantly. "The inspector will be glad to hear it."

"Who would have thought," demanded the foreman of the world at large, "that anyone would have wanted to use a great thing like that for safe-breaking?"

"Someone thought of it," said Crosby. Larky Nolson hadn't been the only criminal to have had trouble with a safe in their manor.

The foreman shrugged his shoulders. "There are always more ways than one of killing the canary."

"It got it open all right," rejoined the constable. "By the time we got here there was money everywhere."

"If we were to drop you from that height onto a spot of hardstanding," said the foreman, "I daresay you'd break open too."

"Yes," said Crosby simply. The manifold highly unpleasant ways in which various members of the police force had died in the course of the execution of their duty was one of the many facts that they impressed on them at their training college. There was a book, too, where they turned over a page every day. . . . He pulled out his notebook. "I'm looking for a man. . . ."

"I didn't think you were just passing the time of day."

"Name of Nicholas Petforth. Tallish. Auburn hair."

"Nick? He was around." The foreman waved an arm. "Ask at the office."

"I did."

"Well?"

"They said he was this way."

"Doesn't look as if he is, does it?"

"No," said Crosby literally. "Can't say it does."

"Well, he was around then." The foreman pushed his cap to the back of his head. "Could he have heard that you were asking for him?"

"Might have done." Crosby coughed delicately. "The word does get around."

"Then," said the foreman, "he probably didn't stay to argue the toss and you've probably gone and lost me the only person who can drive that damned thing over there properly."

The constable followed his gaze towards an enormous earth-moving machine that looked like some grotesque mechanised caterpillar with extra, articulated jaws.

"Watch out," said Crosby solemnly, "that someone doesn't borrow that to dig up the Bank of England."

* * *

Smell is undoubtedly the most evocative of all the senses. At least, Detective Inspector Sloan would have been prepared to swear that it was the moment that he set foot inside the Berebury District General Hospital again. The hospital had that peculiar aroma compounded of as many ingredients as a witch's brew—and very nearly as unsavoury—that seemed to be common to all such institutions. It was one, he decided, that you forgot as you left it but remembered pretty speedily as you stepped over the threshold again.

He went in through the main entrance of the hospital and set about making his way to the pathologist's office. As he did so he lifted his head to take another look at the signs supposed to guide patients in the direction in which they wanted to go. He revised that sentiment almost immediately to "the direction in which they *needed* to go." He could not imagine anyone actually wanting to go to Isolation (a solid unbroken white ring with blankness inside).

He paused briefly under a symbol that represented a man leaning forward on one leg, the other thrust out behind him. The man could have stood for a ballet dancer or a skater. What he couldn't have represented was any medical or surgical speciality that Sloan could possibly think of. He moved on, hurrying past the sign that clearly indicated the nursery. This was three doll-like babies, side by side, wrapped papoose style. "Triplets," he thought in horror to himself, lowering his eyes and quickening his pace. It was a contingency he was not even prepared to begin to contemplate, and he turned off the main corridor as soon as he could.

His mind, though, stayed with the subject of hospital signs. The Mortuary didn't have one. The solitary giant tear-shaped symbol that could have fooled someone seeking that department (or tea and sympathy?) turned out to represent not a human tear but a drop of blood steering the way to the Blood Bank. Nothing representational marked out the Mortuary. He said as much to Dr. Dabbe as he entered his office.

"It's a nice thought," said that worthy. "The forensic equivalent of the good old barber's pole. What do you suggest?"

"Well . . ."

"Something simple?"

"Naturally."

"Skull and crossbones?"

"Too Captain Hook," objected Sloan.

"Ah, Sloan, you've been boning up on pantomime with the baby coming."

"There's the empty skull. What about that?" Sloan couldn't have said why it was that he suddenly felt so light-hearted: perhaps because the death of Beatrice Wansdyke had turned into a proper case after all.

"The 'Alas, poor Yorick' style?" said Dabbe. "Yes, that would do, Sloan, though I rather care for the French pattern myself."

"The French?"

"They have something rather discouraging in red enamel labelled 'Morte' halfway up their electricity pylons."

"Do they?" One day he would travel, of course. His child would need to be shown the world.

"The mediaevalists," Dabbe informed him, warming to the theme, "favoured a death's head as an emblem of mortality."

"Sounds appropriate."

"Especially if there was a moral attached."

"There was always a moral attached in those days."

"True. But if you want to be really modern . . ."

"Most people do," said Sloan inaccurately.

"Then I think I should recommend death ritualised twentieth-century style."

"How?" Sloan cast his mind around the possibilities. There were plenty of them.

"From the Wild West . . ."

Sloan had forgotten that the pathologist was an armchair cowboy.

"A smoking gun would do nicely," pronounced Dabbe. He stood up. "In the meantime, Sloan, we shall have to make do with what signs we've got, shan't we? Come through. . . ."

Sloan followed the pathologist from his office through a door marked quite clearly Medico-Legal Department.

"A nice touch for those of our subjects still able to read," remarked Dabbe. "This way—what we want is in the laboratory."

Seating the detective inspector on a stool in front of a bench, the pathologist reached for a series of little bottles. Less confidently, Sloan reached for his notebook.

"Beatrice Wansdyke died from the effects of diabetes," said the pathologist. "That still holds. She probably had all the symptoms—you'll be able to check on that. She certainly had all the signs, including dehydration. We got as far as that at the post-mortem yesterday."

"Yes."

"What I would have expected to find was some indication in the post-mortem blood-sugar levels that she'd had some insulin not so long before death."

"And you didn't?"

"I didn't." The pathologist pulled a sheet of paper along the bench and then started looking for a particular test tube in a long row in a rack. His hand hovered over them. "There's a fortune waiting for the man who can invent a foolproof way of keeping laboratory specimens attached to their pathological notes."

"And for the discoverer of a perfect jury system," said Sloan feelingly. "Every copper who's ever lived could have done with that."

"These two seem to match," said Dabbe, comparing two separate sets of numbers. "Anyway, this blood-sugar level is far too high for her to have been within shouting distance of a dose of insulin for days."

"Interesting," said Sloan cautiously.

"She also had heavy glycosuria."

"That'll have to keep for the expert witnesses," said Sloan, making a lay attempt at writing it down.

"And ketonuria."

Sloan wrote that down too. After a fashion.

"It all adds up to the same thing," said the pathologist.

"She didn't have her insulin when she should have done?"

"Exactly."

"So?"

"So either she stopped taking it," said the doctor.

"Or," said the policeman, "something or someone kept it from her."

"Medico . . ." began Sloan.

"Or legal," finished Dabbe.

"Difficult."

"Those are the only two inferences that I can draw, too," said the pathologist amiably. "And I shall be quite happy to say so in a court of law."

"Either way it didn't do her any good."

"Either way it killed her," said Dr. Dabbe unequivocably.

"She died of it," nodded Sloan.

"How it came about the way it did is your department, Sloan. Not mine. *Post hoc, ergo propter hoc* as we say in the post-mortem room."

Sloan stood up. Medical Latin was one thing. When the pathologist took to quoting classical tags it was time to go. "Thank you, Doctor."

"You know, Sloan," he said negligently as they crossed the room, "I think after all we only need the one notice here in our department."

Sloan followed the direction of the doctor's bony finger as it pointed to a sign above the door.

"Exit?" he said.

"It says it all," murmured Dr. Dabbe, "doesn't it?"

* * *

Miss Simpson sighed and pressed the bell for her secretary.

"Show them in," she sighed.

Once upon a time the headmistress of the Berebury Grammar School for Girls would have been seriously disturbed at the news that the police had arrived at the school and wished to see her. Not any more. The motor car had put an end to that. So many of the sixth form had their own cars these days that brushes with the law were commonplace.

And if it wasn't the motor car as often or not it was the lure of the great unknown. Time was when girls seldom left home alone. Nowadays even schools like hers had pupils who absconded. Improbable as it seemed, it was one of the drawbacks of the single-sex school.

Miss Simpson had her spiel on this theme practically word-perfect these days. The bolder spirits in a "girls only" school, she would insist to the school governors, were practically certain to find trouble. The quiet girl from a sheltered background in a little village, she would remind startled parents who were on their way to being overprotective, was almost always at even greater risk.

"And Gretna Green," she would say ominously to both groups, "is the only Scottish place name that they all know."

As always, Miss Walsh, the deputy head, agreed with her.

"There is nothing," ran Miss Simpson's favourite sermon to Miss Walsh, "like seeing spotty boys all day and every day for keeping a girl in touch with reality."

The deputy head, who cherished a secret passion for Omar Sharif and who read romantic novels in the privacy of her own bedroom, would nod sagely at this dictum too—but still call in at the library on her chaste way home.

"A gipsy caravan," she said wistfully to the head now. "That's what I set my heart on when I was young. Dear me, how we all do grow up."

"Really!" exclaimed Miss Simpson. "You should have known better than that even then." She looked at the door expectantly. "Let's hope it's not drugs this time, anyway. It will be one day, you know."

"The lure of another great unknown," said little Miss Walsh incorrigibly.

It soon transpired that it wasn't drugs or missing pupils or motor cars that the police wanted to see Miss Simpson about.

It wasn't even about a girl.

"Miss Collins?" said Miss Simpson, puzzled. "Miss Hilda Collins?"

"Miss Wansdyke's friend," said Detective Inspector Sloan.

"Our biologist," said Miss Simpson.

"In the lab," said Miss Walsh, consulting a timetable. "With the fourth form."

The fourth form at Berebury Grammar School for Girls clearly found the visit from an unknown male more exciting than the study of the life cycle of the dog fish upon which they were engaged when he arrived. Miss Hilda Collins, however, was equally the possessor of a lion tamer's eye. One swift look round the laboratory from her and the fourth form had turned its attention back to *Scyllium canicula*.

Detective Inspector Sloan said he was sorry about the death of her friend.

"You shouldn't ever feel sorry for anyone who dies suddenly," said Miss Collins gruffly, pulling herself up and straightening her white coat.

Sloan, who in his time had felt very sorry indeed for a number of people who had died with startling suddenness—mostly as victims—nevertheless knew exactly what she meant and did not argue.

"We don't let domestic and agricultural animals linger," said the biologist, "do we?"

"Not if we can help it," agreed Sloan, his mind turning unbidden to a dead Airedale.

"Then we shouldn't let humans," said Miss Collins trenchantly. She led him to a little office at one end of the laboratory that was above and apart from the class, and then turned and looked him squarely in the eye. "Now, what do you want from me?"

"When did you last see Beatrice Wansdyke?"

"Thursday afternoon," said Hilda Collins without hesitation. "We had a cup of tea together in the staff room after school finished. At least I had a cup. She had three. She said she seemed to be very thirsty all the time."

"Not Friday?"

"I didn't come in to school on Friday. I'd had a bit

of a cold and lost my voice." She twisted her lips wryly. "It's the one faculty that you can't do without in this job."

"And how was Miss Wansdyke on Thursday?" enquired Sloan, making a mental note.

"Not well," said Hilda Collins immediately. "She hadn't been at all well lately. I—we'd—all begun to get a bit worried about her. And so had she, I think. She wondered if she might have picked up some disease while she was in France."

If that noted xenophobe Superintendent Leeyes had been present he, too, would have tried to blame the French first.

"She went with a school party on a tour of the châteaux of the Loire in the summer holidays, you know, Inspector."

Detective Inspector Sloan, who had seen for himself that "Calais" was not engraved on Miss Wansdyke's heart—or anywhere else—and who knew about the absence of insulin in her bloodstream, saw no occasion for blaming the French.

"But the doctor said not," went on the biologist. "He just told her to step up her dose of insulin."

"Quite," said Sloan, keeping silent on the highly germane fact that her friend had died without a trace of it in her body.

"I'm glad she went quickly," said Miss Collins with such fervour that Sloan looked up.

He hadn't, so far in his police working life, encountered a "mercy killing" but there was always a first time.

"I'm a member of a euthanasia society," she said.

Sloan was not surprised.

"When my time comes," averred the schoolteacher, "I shall take something."

Sloan nodded. A lot of people said that they weren't prepared to wait for Death the Reaper. But they usually did.

"Tell me a little about Miss Wansdyke," invited Sloan. He needed to fill out the curiously empty picture of a chemistry mistress that was all he had so far. "Had she any hobbies, for instance?"

Miss Collins considered this. "Just the one."

"Ah."

"More of a passion than a hobby."

"People get like that," said Sloan. Other people, of course. Growing roses well was just a relaxation as far as he was concerned, naturally.

"Everyone has to have something."

"The dog?" he offered tentatively.

The biologist shook her head. "No, no. Not Isolde. No, Beatrice was looking for something."

Sloan waited.

"Everyone has their Holy Grail," she said.

"We're all seekers after something," he advanced in his turn. He was old enough now to know that. With some it was the Truth: but not with everyone. "What was Miss Wansdyke looking for, Miss Collins?"

"A way of using the nitrogen that's present in the air," said Hilda Collins unexpectedly. "She felt that it ought to be possible to convert it."

"Oh," said Sloan blankly.

Miss Collins took pity on him. "It would be a sort of latter-day turning of stone into gold. They tried that a lot in the Middle Ages."

"I see."

"Poor Beatrice," said Hilda Collins. "She never did find it."

"Where did she look?" he asked. "Or rather, where did she do the looking?" Air, after all, was free.

The biologist smiled. "She used to use the laboratories down at Wansdyke and Darnley. At weekends. They didn't mind. She'd done more than her bit for the family."

"So I'm told."

"Perhaps," added Miss Collins abruptly, "her nephew will come to his senses now."

"Nicholas Petforth?"

"Not a bad boy," pronounced the schoolteacher judiciously.

The phrase had long ago lost its meaning to anyone who had spent any time at all in a juvenile court.

"His trouble, Inspector, is that he spends all his time being afraid that he's taking after his father."

"It does happen," advanced Sloan cautiously. He had every intention of his son—if the baby should be a boy—taking after him. Or else.

"Nature not nurture?" murmured the biologist quizzically.

"Well . . ."

"Or nurture not nature?"

"A bit of both," comprised Sloan. He was going to see that that child of his—theirs—when it came was going to be brought up properly too.

"But then you're a policeman, aren't you?" She shot him an intelligent look.

"As the twig is bent," Sloan came back.

"It works with the right-handed thread clockwise honeysuckle," conceded the biologist with a glint of humour, "and the left-handed thread anti-clockwise bindweed."

"If you start it in the right way," said the policeman, who was also a gardener.

"Homo sapiens don't keep all the rules," observed Hilda Collins with profundity.

"There are those," proffered Sloan, "who say, 'Give me a boy until he's seven . . .'"

"And," responded Miss Collins, "those who say that the sins of the fathers are visited upon the sons."

"Even unto the third and fourth generation," finished Sloan. His mother had been most particular about his biblical education.

Miss Collins suddenly looked through the office window. "Turn the scalpel the other way, Veronica," she called out. "You'll never dissect anything with the blunt side. Go on, child! Cut! It won't bite you, you know. It's quite dead." She turned back to Sloan. "Where was I?"

"Heredity, I think, miss."

"Fathers," said Hilda Collins, looking Sloan up and down, "only amount to half the genetic programme."

Sloan had never considered paternity in quite that light before and said so.

"Though," remarked Miss Collins academically, "in some ways the rhesus monkey's father is of relatively little importance."

Detective Inspector Sloan said nothing. He had always in any case been on the side of the angels anyway. Apes were less appealing.

"The little woman," said the biologist, following a completely different line of thought, "does her share, too."

"Er—quite so," said Sloan, making up his mind there and then that Margaret, his wife, was not going to hear about this interview at all. Some aspects of police work were not for home consumption.

"There was nothing wrong with Nicholas Petforth's mother, I can assure you." Miss Collins plunged her hands deeply into the pockets of her white coat. "Young Briony's her living image."

"Nature not nurture," said Sloan neatly.

She acknowledged this with a quick jerk of her head. "And there'll be nothing wrong with the boy when he stops running away from himself."

"It would help," observed Sloan mildly, "if he stopped running away from us."

"Like that, is it?" She raised ungroomed eyebrows heavenwards: and then turned away from him again. "Deeper, Veronica! Cut deeper. . . ."

For his money, thought Sloan, Miss Hilda Collins could have slit the throats of a whole pack of dogs.

Chapter 9

My eyes are bleared with work on preparations,
That's all the good you get from transmutations.

"Just a few enquiries, Doctor," began Detective Inspector Sloan. The general practitioner's consulting room was a much less intimidating place than the hospital. There were no white coats about and precious few instruments visible. The chairs and the desk were more homely, too. Detective Constable Crosby was sitting in the chair that was slightly behind and to one side of the doctor's direct line of vision and was presumably the one intended for the patient's friend or relative. Sloan himself was occupying the patient's chair, facing the doctor.

Dr. John Paston regarded him straightly across the desk. "About what, Inspector?"

"The late Miss Beatrice Wansdyke."

"Ah, yes. Of course, Inspector." The general practitioner relaxed almost imperceptibly: but Sloan noticed. Few people realised to what extent body signs gave them away. And that those signs were the more revealing just because they were usually completely uncontrived. Even a professional straight-face like Dr. Paston was not able to conceal them completely. And the professional watcher of people across the desk from him duly took note.

"She was one of your patients, I believe," said Detective Inspector Sloan, realising, when he came to think about it, that this matter of understanding and portraying body language was one of the main ingredients of really first-class stage acting.

"Indeed, yes." The doctor pushed a stethoscope to one side. "For many years."

"We understand that she suffered from diabetes."

"That is so."

Sloan was as quick to notice the quality of the response as he had been to notice the body signs. Never to advance more information than was requested was the hallmark of the skilled interviewee. The doctor was the sort of witness who would stand up well to cross-examination in court. There was no spilling over of extraneous detail here: nothing to give an interrogator a handle.

"Long-standing?" said Sloan.

"Very."

"How did she cope?"

This at least elicited a slightly more expanded reply from the general practitioner.

"Very well, really. She was sensible—that's what matters most in caring for that condition."

Sloan nodded. "She didn't kick over the traces?" It was nice to know that there were other professions which also had to deal with kickers of traces. But if nobody in society ever did step out of line. . . . His wife had read extracts from *Brave New World* to him once. He didn't like the idea of programmed obedience either. He preferred the middle way. One way and another you usually came back to that.

"Let us say," said Dr. Paston, building a steeple with his fingers, "that she was an intelligent woman who understood her condition very well and acted accordingly."

"Not careless?"

"Certainly not."

"And not given to eating what was bad for her?"

"I would have thought, never." He frowned. "She would understand the consequences too well."

"Or missing out her insulin?"

"Out of the question."

"I see."

"She was most punctilious about that. In any case . . ." He paused.

"Yes?"

"In any case," the doctor said more slowly, "if she did forget she would begin to feel ill and that would remind her."

The doctor rearranged a prescription pad and a book of certificates on his desk top while Sloan said quietly, "That's what we thought."

"Besides," continued the general practitioner, "as it happens I had actually advised her to step up her dose the week before she died, not once but twice, so she would scarcely have forgotten. Quite the reverse, I should have said."

"Would it surprise you, Dr. Paston, to know that the pathologist could find no trace whatsoever of insulin at the post-mortem?"

"Very much," said the practitioner vigorously. "In fact, I would find it exceedingly difficult to credit."

"Moreover," continued Sloan, "he also found a number of signs that indicated quite positively that she had not had any insulin for some days before her death."

"I can tell you," countered the doctor immediately, "exactly when she had her last prescription." He flipped a switch and asked a secretary for Beatrice Wansdyke's medical case notes.

"She also had some symptoms indicative of shortage of insulin," went on Sloan firmly. "We have a witness of her being unusually thirsty, for instance, on Thursday."

The doctor's head came up most alertly at that but he did not speak, and there was a sort of silence while they waited for the notes to arrive. Detective Constable Crosby used it to turn over the pages of his notebook slowly and deliberately in such a manner as to emphasise that he was taking notes. Detective Inspector Sloan spent the time studying the general practitioner. He was grey-haired, sparely built, and not—at a guess—very far short of retirement. He gave every appearance at the moment of a puzzled man—but not a frightened one. Dr. Paston himself was clearly using the lead time for thinking hard.

When the patient's notes arrived the situation took a completely new turn.

"As I say," began the doctor, scanning them rapidly,

"Miss Wansdyke consulted me at Thursday evening's surgery last week and I advised extra units of insulin morning and evening. She had ample supplies. Her last prescription was . . ." His face changed. He looked suddenly older. "As it happens," he said carefully, "I didn't write her last prescription. It was given to her in September while I was on holiday."

"Oh?"

"My partner wrote it out for her, as I was away."

"Dr. McCavity?" said Sloan.

"Dr. Peter McCavity?" said Detective Constable Crosby from the patient's friend's chair in a manner which betokened prior acquaintance with the name.

"Perhaps, Dr. Paston," suggested Sloan, "if we might just check with him?" It would be interesting in any case to see the knocker down of so many items of what the town planners called "street furniture."

"By all means, Inspector," said the doctor without enthusiasm. "I'll ask him to step through."

There was an altogether different cut of jib about the man who came along in response to Dr. Paston's message. He was a much younger man but already his features had taken on the blur of self-indulgence. He positioned himself against the examination couch at the side of the room, a hand resting rather too heavily against it for normal support purposes.

"Police?" he said uncertainly. "If it's about that bollard in the Eastgate yesterday . . ."

"Our Inspector Harpe is dealing with that, Doctor."

"I meant to report it. No time, you know. Urgent medical work."

"You'll be hearing from him in due course," said Sloan formally.

"Oh . . . oh, yes. Thank you." Dr. McCavity managed an acknowledging nod. "Some fool cut in on me. . . ."

There was the accumulation of years of skill and experience in the totally expressionless way in which Sloan contrived to cast doubt on the driver's statement while doing and saying nothing provocative that an astute defence counsel could use in evidence.

"While we're talking about cars, Doctor . . ." began Sloan.

"Go on." Peter McCavity brought his gaze to bear upon the detective inspector but seemed to have some little difficulty in keeping it there.

"Can you tell me where your car was parked on Friday afternoon?"

"Friday?" Now he merely looked bewildered. "Last Friday?"

"Last Friday," said Sloan patiently. For the young doctor last Friday was clearly light-years away from this Wednesday morning.

An expression of genuine puzzlement came over his prematurely blunted features. "Friday? I should have to think about that. When on Friday?"

"Afternoon turning to evening."

"Friday was a long time ago."

"I daresay."

"With the weekend in between." He made the weekend sound as solid as the house but for which you could see to Hackney Marshes ("wiv a ladder and some glasses").

"It's easy to lose a weekend," agreed Sloan temperately. In fact "lost" weekends were quite a feature of a certain condition.

"My weekend off," said McCavity.

"I see, sir."

"Not on duty."

"I understand."

"Very tired."

"Quite."

"I didn't feel very well on Friday."

"I see, sir."

He looked around unsurely. "I may have had a little sleep in my car."

"Can you remember whereabouts, sir?"

The doctor roused himself to a modicum of belligerence. "Nothing wrong with that, is there, Inspector?"

"No, sir. Not in itself."

"Well?"

"Would you have been anywhere near Ridley Road?"

His aggression collapsed as speedily as a pricked balloon. His face changed pathetically. "Oh, my God, Inspector!" He clutched Sloan's sleeve in an alarmed manner. "I didn't . . . don't tell me that I"—his whole frame shuddered—"I haven't knocked anyone down, have I?"

His senior partner, Dr. John Paston, stirred at last behind his desk and said brusquely, "Oughtn't you to be cautioning him, Inspector?"

"I don't think so, Doctor," replied Sloan evenly. He knew his Judge's Rules as well as the next policeman and he didn't need any spectator—or even the referee, come to that—telling him he was off-side.

"What is all this anyway?" demanded Dr. McCavity. "This isn't a police state yet, you know."

"Just a few questions, sir, that's all."

"More like the third degree," complained the young doctor bitterly. His words would have carried more conviction without the fine tremor of his hands that shouldn't have been present in one so young.

"It's a wise man that knows his own movements," said Sloan prosaically. "Were you near Ridley Road on Friday afternoon?"

He hesitated. "I may have been."

Sloan turned back to Dr. Paston. "Perhaps we might ask Dr. McCavity instead if he can remember writing Miss Wansdyke's prescription for insulin while you were away."

The young doctor answered for himself. "That'll be down in black and white, Inspector. You'll be able to see that for yourself." He turned scornfully to a stony-faced Dr. Paston. "Wansdyke? That's the old bird who's left you some money, isn't it?"

* * *

"Well," demanded Superintendent Leeyes, "where are we now?"

Detective Inspector Sloan had reported to his superior's office as soon as he got back to the police station. If it hadn't been for the feminine overtones of the simile, he thought privately, you could have likened the superintendent to a queen bee placed firmly in the centre of her hive. What with worker bees reporting back all day honey-laden, other bees dancing attendance upon the queen bee (there was no shortage of lady clerical workers servicing the superintendent's out basket and telephone line), and sentry bees on guard duty at the mouth of the hive, the organisation of the police station at Berebury could have changed places with a beehive any day.

"How far have you got, Sloan?"

Except, of course, that there were no drones in the Calleshire Force.

"Sloan, are you listening?"

"Yes, sir," he said, pulling himself together quickly. Ants were known to be well organised, too. "We haven't made a lot of headway so far."

"You've had all morning."

"Yes, sir." There was no doubt either, thought Sloan confusedly to himself, about who was top dog in their hive, so to speak.

"Found the nephew yet?"

"No, sir."

"Got a general call out for him?"

"A whisper," replied Sloan, "has gone around the nebulae."

"What's that, Sloan?"

"Nothing, sir. Sorry, sir." He brought his mind back smartly to the here and now by getting out his notebook and opening it in front of him. "We're looking for Nicholas Petforth now."

Leeyes grunted. "You saw the pathologist . . ."

"He's quite certain, sir, that the deceased didn't have her insulin."

"And her general practitioner?"

"He's quite certain, sir, that she did." There was some elusive quotation hovering about in his mind about when doctors differ but he couldn't pin it down. "Or rather . . ."

"Yes?"

"He's quite sure that she wouldn't have stopped taking it."

Leeyes grunted again. "So?"

"So there remains the alternative that she thought she was taking it."

"You mean that when she gave herself an injection it wasn't insulin?"

"It figures," said Sloan cautiously.

"It didn't do her any good," agreed Leeyes grimly, "did it, whatever it was she had instead?"

"No. We know she wasn't feeling well on it. That's why the doctor told her to increase the dose."

"Compounding the error," pronounced the superintendent neatly.

"Er—quite, sir." The depths of the superintendent's knowledge and ignorance were equally unfathomable to his subordinates. They couldn't count on either. "Increasing the dose didn't help, you see."

"And it should have done, I take it?"

"Oh, yes. In theory, anyway. That's why Dr. Paston upped the dose again after that."

"Or said that he did, Sloan," warned the superintendent.

"Yes, sir. Naturally." That went without saying at this stage. There was always an unwritten and unspoken caveat in all police work acknowledging the difference between what was given in an untried statement and what was offered—tested—in evidence.

"Putting the dose up yet again didn't help either, of course," observed Leeyes.

"No, sir."

"Nothing and nothing is still nothing."

"It reinforces the theory that what she gave herself wasn't insulin." Sloan, who was no mathematician, shifted his ground slightly. "According to the medical men, her symptoms should have gone away on the bigger dose."

"Not got worse, like they did."

"No."

"Sloan, I don't like the sound of this."

"No, sir."

"Someone wanted that woman dead,"

"There could have been an accident," pointed out Sloan, for form's sake as much as anything. "A duff supply or something like that."

Leeyes gave a Machiavellian smile. "Putting the whole thing down to bad luck, are you, Sloan?"

"No, sir, but . . ."

"And the quarter of a million pounds to good luck?"

"Never, sir . . ." He meant that. The one thing he didn't want any child of his to have was unlimited wealth on the grand scale. He didn't call that good luck.

"And," carried on the superintendent, pursuing his own line of thought, "as for having the bad luck to have a fatal accident at the same time as having the good luck to have come by a large sum of money . . ."

"Unlikely," agreed Sloan. The Furies usually went so far and no further. Not that you could count on that either.

"One in the eye for Yin and Yang."

"Beg pardon, sir?"

"The unity of opposites."

"Er—quite, sir." Sloan quickly racked his brains. The superintendent attended adult education classes in his spare time. Indiscriminately. One way and another they had all left their mark on the force.

"Equal and opposite, you might say."

"Indeed, yes, sir." Was that, Sloan wondered, a hangover from Mathematics for All and congruent triangles or Eastern Philosophies for Enquiring Minds?"

"Someone," repeated Leeyes forcefully, "wanted that woman dead."

"Yes, sir." He cleared his throat. "If we accept that then I rather think that we can go a little further than that."

"Come on then . . . don't just sit there, man! Tell me."

"I think someone wanted her dead sooner rather than later."

The superintendent shot Sloan a shrewd look from under his bushy eyebrows. "We've got a speedy Gonzales about, have we?"

"It would be possible to argue, sir," said Sloan, picking his words with care, "that withholding the insulin wasn't doing the trick quickly enough for someone."

"Would it, indeed," said Leeyes discouragingly.

"There's the dog, you see, sir."

"The dead dog," said Leeyes.

"The missing dog," Sloan corrected him. "I reckon that the missing dog was meant to be the last straw."

"On top of everything else. I see." He paused. "You think that even without insulin she was taking too long to die?"

"Too long for someone's comfort. Yes."

"What was the hurry?"

"I don't know," said Sloan uneasily.

"What had she got to be got out of the way in time for, then?" he said, putting it another way.

"I don't know that either, sir."

"Something that has already happened?" he mused.

"Or," said Sloan warily, "something that is going to happen?" That was always the policeman's especial nightmare: the spur that kept the officer on the job long after people in other occupations had gone home for the night.

Leeyes leant back in his chair, considering that. "Is there any hurry about the girl Briony Petforth's marriage to the registrar fellow?"

"Not that I know about."

"Times have changed," said the superintendent obscurely.

"Yes, sir." It was something that would have to be gone into, all the same.

"Your wife all right, by the way?" enquired Leeyes gruffly.

"Yes, thank you, sir." Sloan kept his voice even with an effort. The superintendent's patently obvious thought processes didn't need a Sigmund Freud on hand with explanation. They never had. "But," Sloan continued vigorously, "if there's anything suspicious about Dr. Roger Elspin I can tell you one thing, and that's that he's not going to have anything to do with my wife's confinement—obstetrical register or not—even if"—he searched wildly around in his mind for alternatives—"even if I have to deliver her myself."

"Don't tempt Providence," advised Leeyes soberly. "Remember that every policeman in his time . . ."

"Yes, sir. Of course, sir." Sloan let his pent-up feeling evaporate and came back to the case in hand. And the beehive. "Miss Wansdyke, sir . . . where shall we go for honey?"

"What's that, Sloan?"

"Ridley Road, sir. That's where I'm going now."

Chapter 10

The slippery science stripped me down so bare
That I'm worth nothing, here or anywhere.

"Mr. Wansdyke will see you now, Inspector." A young secretary turned back from the telephone switchboard at her reception desk. "It's the second door on the left."

The first door had Malcolm Darnley's name on it. It was open and the room empty.

George Wansdyke's office was the next one to it. Two men who had been in there talking to the businessman slid unobtrusively towards the door as he and Crosby approached.

"Our Mr. Carruthers," Wansdyke introduced them briefly, "the head progress chaser . . ."

Detective Inspector Sloan acknowledged the introduction with interest. They weren't short of progress chasers down at the station, though there they went under slightly different names. Like "the press" and "the chief constable."

". . . and," went on Wansdyke, "Bill Benfleet, advertising and public relations executive."

The public relations man immediately gave Sloan a hearty professional handshake. "We'll be straight back, Mr. Wansdyke," he said over his shoulder. "That press release has got to be done today whatever happens." He waved another acknowledgement at Crosby and gave a quick meaningless smile to George Wansdyke. "Time and tide and newspapers wait for no man."

"Welcome, Inspector." Wansdyke motioned Sloan and Crosby into chairs that were considerably more comfortable than the ones in either the doctor's surgery

or the hospital. The man seemed more confident in his
office than he had been at home. Sloan could understand this. Mrs. Pauline Wansdyke's propensity for not
letting any time elapse between thought and speech
must be unnerving.

"Thank you, sir."

"Sorry about the unfortunate aroma."

Detective Constable Crosby raised his head like a
pointer and sniffed the air.

Sloan's mind went back to his childhood. "Car-
bolic?" he hazarded.

"We've just taken delivery of some phenol," Wansdyke explained. "It's one of the commonest components
we use. That and the aldehydes."

Crosby lowered his nose again, like a bloodhound
this time.

"The smell seems to get into everything." Wansdyke was apologetic.

"Plastic," said Sloan. "That's what you manufacture
here, sir, isn't it?"

"It is," said Wansdyke, nodding assent. "We go in
for the more rarefied varieties these days but"—he
pointed across the room—"time was when we didn't."

The two policemen followed his gaze to an early set
of crudely moulded red products in plastic laid out in a
display cabinet. Crosby sniffed.

"That's what we made in my father's day. They're
practically museum pieces now."

Crosby looked doubtful.

"We've come a long way since then technically and
aesthetically," Wansdyke assured him.

"Plastic's never exactly beautiful, is it, sir?" interposed Sloan diplomatically before the constable could
speak.

Wansdyke gave a short laugh. "I don't know about
that but I do know the world would have a job to get by
without it now."

"It did before," remarked Crosby mulishly.

"I suppose the end product is getting better all the
time," said Sloan hastily, though surely he had read
somewhere, hadn't he, that what really mattered was a
better mousetrap.

"Research." Wansdyke nodded. "We do a lot of that here, Inspector."

"Your aunt was doing some, too, sir, wasn't she?" Sloan trawled the remark in front of Wansdyke.

He wasn't sure what it was that he had expected by way of response. Perhaps the half-deprecating indulgence that grown men usually showed to aunts. George Wansdyke's reaction to what Sloan had said however was totally serious.

"She was indeed. On a most interesting hypothesis, Inspector."

Sloan waited. Everyone had a different way of describing his own particular crock of gold that lay where the rainbow ended.

"Recovering nitrogen from the atmosphere was what she was aiming at—no less," said the businessman.

Sloan cleared his throat. "A worthy goal, sir."

"A great step forward for mankind. That's what my partner—Malcom Darnley—you may have heard of him, Inspector?"

Sloan nodded.

"He's devoted to conservation, you know."

Had Inspector Harpe been present he would no doubt have ground his teeth. Sloan contented himself with admitting that he knew Malcolm Darnley by reputation.

"Well, he feels so strongly about these things that he too was quite happy to let Beatrice use our laboratory facilities at the weekend."

"And had she found it—what she was looking for?"

"The sixty-four thousand dollar question, you might say," observed Crosby easily from the sidelines.

Sloan drew breath to speak. That was *lèse-majesté*, pure and simple.

"If she had," said Wansdyke lightly, "she hadn't told me."

"Your research . . ."

"Tied up with development," said the businessman. "Ours and other people's. There doesn't seem to be any danger of people not wanting synthetic resins for the rest of my lifetime, and my son's either."

Running out of crime was one thing they didn't have

to worry about down at the police station. There'd be plenty for his son to take care of, too. If he had a son.

Crosby started on another objection. "But . . ."

"At least," intervened Sloan hastily, "plastic lasts. Not like some things these days."

"Quite," said George Wansdyke briskly. He straightened the blotter on his desk. "Now what can I do for you two gentlemen?"

"What we'd really like, sir," said Sloan frankly, "is the key to your aunt's house."

"Oh?"

"Something's—er—turned up."

"What?"

"Her dog."

"How?" asked Wansdyke, startled.

"Dead."

"Good Lord."

"Dead and buried, actually."

"Beatrice must have found it herself then," said Wansdyke, relaxing.

"Must she, sir?"

"We looked for it everywhere after . . . when . . . after we found Beatrice."

"Did you, sir? It was in the garden."

"We thought it must have just run away."

"No," said Sloan thoughtfully, "I don't think that's what happened." His grandmother had been enough of a sentimentalist to have a copy of Sir Edwin Landseer's painting of a dog called "The Old Shepherd's Chief Mourner" in her front parlour. It had made a great impression on him as a small child.

"We were afraid it was hungry or frightened," said Wansdyke. "Briony was quite worried in case it was suffering."

"It didn't seem to have suffered a lot," replied Sloan tangently.

"Good. What with poor Beatrice herself . . ."

"Quite."

"It never rains but it pours, doesn't it?" observed Crosby chattily.

Wansdyke turned his gaze towards the detective constable. "That's true."

"So," said Sloan, rising to his feet, "we thought we would just check that everything was all in order round there, if that's all right with you, sir."

"Of course." The businessman felt in his pocket for the keys. "The electricity and water are off at the main but not the gas."

* * *

"Nurse! Nurse! Nurse Petforth . . ."

"Coming."

"Nurse!"

"What is it?"

"Sister wants you."

Briony Petforth straightened her cap in a purely reflex action before she looked round. "Where is she?"

One of Sister Fleming's most notable administrative qualities was that of always seeming able to materialise anywhere on the ward without warning.

"Her office."

Briony automatically smoothed her apron as she hurried there.

"A telephone call for you, Nurse," said Sister Fleming, oozing disapproval. "It should not be necessary for me to have to remind you that nurses on duty are not expected to receive telephone calls."

"No, Sister."

"Except of an urgent personal nature about family matters."

"Yes, Sister."

"The caller," she said, "insists on speaking to you."

"Thank you, Sister."

Sister Fleming gave her a curious look and handed over the telephone receiver.

"Briony?" said a man's voice. "Is that you? This is George Wansdyke."

"Yes?" she said cautiously. Sister Fleming was sitting at her desk only inches away.

"Look here, I've just had the police round at the office asking for the key of Ridley Road." Wansdyke lowered his voice. "I've given it to them naturally, but I'm worried about Nick."

"Yes," she said dully, "so am I."

"He's disappeared from his job on the motorway site. I checked."

"I know," she said miserably.

"And as far as I can make out from the layabouts there he's left that dreadful squat in Luston, too."

"I expect he's sleeping rough again," she said without thinking.

Sister Fleming lifted her head.

"Or else he's found somewhere else to stay," she added hastily.

"And," added Wansdyke, "they've found the dog."

"Isolde!" exclaimed Briony. "Where?"

"Buried in the garden," said George Wansdyke.

"Buried in the garden!" cried Briony. "Dead, you mean?"

Sister Fleming's eyebrows almost reached her starched cap.

"Dead, I do mean," said Wansdyke grimly.

"But who . . . how . . . why?"

Sister Fleming wasn't even troubling to conceal her interest now.

"I don't know," said Wansdyke, "and I don't want to start guessing."

* * *

Detective Inspector Sloan had not expected to be back at the hospital again quite so soon. This time he had Detective Constable Crosby with him.

"Which way, sir?"

"Ah," murmured Sloan, "you have a point there. Think of the place as a maze with a man in the middle—a man we want to talk to. His name is Elspin—Dr. Roger Elspin."

Miss Wansdyke's house in Ridley Road had been unrevealing. Neat and tidy but unyielding of clues to a quarter of a million pounds. And no ransom notes had been immediately visible—for the dog or anyone else. He was momentarily tempted to wonder if Ted Blake's wife had made a mistake in what she had overheard—

until he remembered the absent insulin. Dr. Dabbe didn't make mistakes.

"There's an enquiry desk over there, sir," said Crosby.

There was also an exceedingly attractive young receptionist sitting at it.

"No," said Sloan thoughtfully, "I think not."

Verbal enquiries for a doctor by members of the constabulary on duty seldom did that doctor's reputation any good. Besides, Sloan was as curious as the next man. He wanted to see where the symbolic direction signs got Crosby.

"We could have him called," suggested the detective constable, whose own personal radio was a perpetual anathema to him. "Let Big Brother find him for us."

"We'll find him ourselves," said Sloan decisively, "and then we'll have a nice quiet chat."

"Quiet, sir? Here?"

The constable had a point. The one thing the hospital wasn't was quiet.

"They could do with their 'Hospital—Quiet Please' sign inside here," remarked Crosby. "Not out on the road."

"It isn't there," remarked Sloan. "Not any more."

"Our Dr. McCavity been out for a drive then?" enquired Crosby.

"Friendly neighbourhood students, Inspector Harpe thought," replied Sloan absently. "Souvenir hunting." The ways of students remained obscure to him. "This way, I think."

The constable, though, seemed curiously reluctant to move away from the hospital's entrance concourse. "What, sir, if anyone asks us who we are?"

Sloan, who made a point of wearing clothes as unremarkable as those of the next man, looked Crosby up and down. The constable's wearing apparel tended to be influenced by the silver screen. Sloan drew a breath. "Representatives from a pharmaceutical company, I think." Then he caught sight of Crosby's trendy tie and added drily, "One of the lesser firms, I should say myself. Now, come on."

Crosby looked up at the daunting array of signs—

and perversely spotted a notice that Sloan had never seen at all.

"What do they do at the Gut Club, sir?"

"I have no idea," said Sloan icily.

"On Fridays at nine," added Crosby gratuitously.

"We are here on duty."

Crosby looked around. "Do we have to wait until the lights go down or can we start straightaway?"

"What we have to do," said Sloan with some acerbity, "is to find the obstetrical registrar."

Crosby said, "Lead on, MacDuff," but he said it to Sloan's back.

In the end they got to the right department—chiefly by following a pretty young nurse.

"She might have been going to radiotherapy," objected Sloan. It really was a most unfair world.

"Luck's better than judgement, sir," said Crosby laconically. "Now, where's our man?"

He—Sloan—was definitely not one of those policemen who went in for much reading about police work these days. In his book, practise had overtaken theory years ago. It had been different when he had been plain Police Constable Sloan and first feeling his way on the beat. Then he had read everything he could lay his hands on and one of the things that he had read then had stayed with him over the years. It had been advice on the easy identification of members of the medical profession.

A certain arrogance, his good book had said, went with the smell of antiseptic.

There was assuredly nothing tentative about Dr. Roger Elspin's manner.

"Yes?" he began peremptorily. Strange men did not often stray into his domain.

"I am Detective Inspector Sloan, Doctor, from Berebury Criminal Investigation Department."

"Well?"

"With a few enquiries."

"You'll have to make them short." Dr. Elspin was not noticeably apprehensive either.

"Yes, Doctor."

Elspin indicated the radio receiver clipped to the

pocket of his white coat. "I'm on call for the delivery ward."

"Big Brother is watching you, too," murmured Crosby almost under his breath.

"Big Sister actually," murmured Elspin wryly.

"I won't keep you long," said Sloan mendaciously. Dr. Elspin's sort of time-saving did not come into police work. Time was not money or anything else when law and order—let alone justice—were concerned.

"Good," said Elspin shortly.

"It's about Miss Wansdyke," said Sloan.

A frown crossed his forehead. "Well?"

"I understand that you and her niece, Miss Briony Petforth, are . . . want to . . ."

"We're not just good friends, Inspector," Elspin cut across his speech brusquely, "if that's what you want to know."

"No, sir?"

"Moreover, old-fashioned as it may seem, we're going to get married in the bargain."

"I see, Doctor." Elspin seemed determined enough to convince Sloan. He didn't know if Briony Petforth had taken any persuading.

"Her aunt tried to stop us," said the young man militantly. "That's the long and the short of that."

"Why?"

"Because Briony hadn't finished her precious training, that's why."

"Ah." Sloan nodded sagely. Training had been precious in the aunt's day and marriage a bar to finishing it. "The generation game."

"What . . . oh, yes, of course." Elspin relaxed slightly. "Beatrice said she should get her nursing registration first."

"I see."

"She was a schoolteacher, you see."

"They tend to think like that," said Sloan.

"The old brigade." Elspin endorsed that with feeling. "They think that every woman should have a career to fall back on."

"Those that haven't," observed Sloan moderately, "have sometimes regretted it."

Elspin wasn't listening. "What did Beatrice think I was going to do? Abandon Briony six months after I'd married her?"

Sloan forbore to answer that. There was no use reminding the impetuous young man that that too had been known to happen to new brides.

"There was something else she would keep harping on," said Elspin morosely.

"What was that?"

"That having a professional qualification," he snapped, "meant that a wife could always keep her independence."

"Ah, yes. Of course." He could see that the old schoolmistress would think like that.

"I shan't stop Briony working if she wants to."

"No, sir," said Sloan readily. "Naturally." He saw no point in exploring the narrow line of demarcation between being a working wife and being a woman with a career. Helping to bring home the bacon before cooking it was something quite different from being a career woman in one's own right. Roger Elspin would find that out soon enough.

"She'd only just started her third year," said Elspin, a note of grievance creeping into his voice.

"So that if the late Miss Wansdyke had had her way," observed Sloan, "you would have had to wait nearly another year from now?"

"And I didn't see why we should," said Elspin.

"Well . . ."

"Just because some old bird who was fifty years behind the times thought it wasn't a good idea."

"No," said Sloan, whose only real concern was whether the doctor had thought so strongly enough to take Draconian action in the matter; action outside the law.

"Beatrice was living in the past," he grumbled.

Sloan would have agreed with that straightaway. There had been nothing too modern about number fifty-nine Ridley Road. Furniture and decor both belonged to an earlier decade, and the Turkey carpet on the upstairs landing to an even older one still. There had been no sign of wealth either. That was what was so odd. Evidence of decent modest prosperity had abounded—and so had signs of care and attention to hearth and home but there had been no indicators that spelt money on a large scale.

"The time to marry," pronounced the young man in white coat sitting in front of him, "is when you feel like it."

"Ah," said Sloan, who was older, "that's as may be."

"So," responded Elspin smartly, "that's establishment heresy now, too, is it?"

"No, Doctor. That's practical politics, that is."

Detective Constable Crosby stirred. "Depends if she'll have you when you feel like marrying, doesn't it, Doctor?"

Sloan cleared his throat authoritatively. This was no time to be discussing *marriage à la mode*. "Dr. Elspin, exactly how much say did Miss Wansdyke have in the matter of her niece's marriage?"

"Taking Miss Petforth's consent for granted, of course," put in Crosby sedulously.

Elspin shot the constable an aggressive look but it was Sloan whom he answered. "None, Inspector." He twisted his lips in a wry smile. "She didn't carry any real clout. . . ."

"Well, then . . ."

"And yet she had the greatest pull of all."

"Which was?"

"An appeal to Briony's better nature."

"I see," said Sloan. And he did. In his experience people's better natures were only ever appealed to for causes that didn't respond to logic or common sense.

"Below the belt," commented Crosby insouciantly.

Sloan drew a savage breath. . . .

"All Beatrice said," remarked Elspin more calmly, "was that she was her aunt and had brought her up after her parents were killed. Naturally Briony didn't want to hurt her feelings. . . ." His irateness seemed to have evaporated now.

"Miss Wansdyke had nothing and everything, didn't she?" agreed Sloan. "Now, sir, if . . ."

That was the moment at which Dr. Elspin's radio receiver came to life.

"Dr. Roger Elspin," intoned in a nasal voice. "Calling Dr. Elspin. To go to room three . . . delivery ward . . . now . . ."

He stood up with a shrug. "By the way, Inspector . . ."

"Yes, Doctor."

"Your name's Sloan, isn't it?"

"It is."

"Got a wife?"

"Yes, Doctor."

"Called Margaret?"

Sloan nodded.

"That's what I thought," said Elspin. He essayed a formal smile. "Then we may meet again."

"Yes, Doctor," said Sloan heavily.

"Soon, perhaps." Elspin waved a hand and was gone.

"I think," said Sloan to Crosby, as they stood in the corridor, "that we could well use another chat with Nurse Briony Petforth."

"What I could use," said the constable, "is food and drink."

"If," said Sloan somewhat maliciously, "you can spot a sign made up of a knife and fork then I think you might be onto something—unless that means surgery."

Crosby pointed to a notice board. "They don't eat there, do they, sir, do you think?"

"Where?"

"The Gut Club."

"I hope not," said Sloan repressively. "This way."

Fleming Ward had not been reduced to a symbol. It proclaimed itself in alphabetical terms from afar and the two policemen had no difficulty in finding the right direction.

"They don't mention distances, though, sir, do they?" grumbled Crosby as one long white corridor belayed into another long white corridor.

"I think we're getting warmer," murmured Sloan. "Slow down a bit."

"Sir?"

"I may be wrong," said Sloan softly, "but I think we may not be the only ones making for Fleming Ward."

"Sir?"

"The man ahead, Crosby . . . the one in the donkey jacket."

"Auburn hair, five foot five, slight build . . ."

"Remind you of anyone?"

"Nicholas Petforth," breathed Crosby.

"Going to see his sister," concluded Sloan neatly.

"Hiding up in the hospital?"

"Nobody's asked us what we're up to yet," said Sloan reasonably.

The man ahead turned to the right and quickened his pace slightly. Sloan and Crosby lengthened their steps.

"One on either side," instructed Sloan quietly, "when I say the word."

They had reckoned though without that primordial sense given even to man to tell him when he is being watched or followed. No sooner had the two policemen started to draw close when the man looked around. As soon as he saw them he began to run.

"After him!" shouted Sloan, starting to give chase.

"He's got freckles," said Crosby.

"Never mind that now. Get him!"

Had that particular corridor been long and straight too the two policemen might have had a better chance of catching the man ahead. Instead their quarry ducked down the next turning and then took the next opening after that. Half a minute later he had put a stretcher case between himself and his pursuers.

Crosby dipped swiftly to one side of porters and patient and shot around the next corner after him shouting, "Hey, you there! Stop!"

If anything, the man put on an extra spurt.

Sloan pelted down the new corridor after him. This one at least was long and straight and Crosby appeared to be gaining on his man. Sloan summoned up his reserves for an extra spurt and prepared to fall upon the man in front when Crosby had caught up with him. His added weight would come in useful then.

And then—quite suddenly—the man they were chasing wasn't anywhere to be seen any more.

He had disappeared abruptly through a pair of swing doors.

To Sloan's surprise, Detective Constable Crosby did

not follow him through them. Instead the younger policeman skidded to a sudden halt.

"What the . . . Crosby!"

The constable straightened up and pointed.

Above the double doors were the unmistakable words "Quarantine Area—Keep Out." And on either side of the doorway there were equally unequivocal signs proclaiming "Bio-activity—Do Not Enter."

Chapter 11

Our furnace too for calcifying action,
Our waters in a state of albefaction.

"What!" bellowed Leeyes. "Do you mean to just stand there and tell me you lost him?"

"We did," said Sloan. Sometimes with the superintendent a short answer stood one in better stead than a long one.

"And what were you afraid of?" snarled Superintendent Leeyes in a transport of rage. "Foot and mouth disease?"

"Quarantine," said Sloan, speaking for himself. Detective Constable Crosby had been muttering about the Black Death.

"He was within your reach. . . ." moaned Leeyes, taking a deep breath.

"But he slipped through our fingers," finished Sloan for him.

Unwisely, as it happened.

"Sloan, this isn't one of your fancy games of cricket. This is for real."

"So is the Bio-activity, sir."

"What does it mean?" asked Leeyes suspiciously.

Sloan, too, had had to ask. "It's the place in the hospital—in the whole of Calleshire, actually—where they keep the cultures of the stuff that they don't want to get out and about. Viruses, mostly."

That hadn't been quite how the administrators had put it to the two policemen but it had been what they had meant.

"Catching," said Leeyes, reducing the matter to its simplest.

"Highly," said Sloan. All the people working in the department there had had head-to-foot white gowns on and masks and there were lots of glass barriers everywhere. "You could see things, sir, but not touch them."

"Supermarkets should be like that," said Leeyes, momentarily diverted. "Save a lot of trouble."

"I gather," offered Sloan, "that there's quite a bit of medical research going on in there too."

"There always is," said Leeyes. "No one ever wants to get on with the actual job these days."

The administrator at the hospital and George Wansdyke of Messrs. Wansdyke and Darnley, plastics specialists, had both spoken more reverently about research but Sloan knew what Leeyes meant. The wellmeaning and the academic had both been researching into crime since Cain killed Abel without coming up with a satisfactory solution.

"So," Sloan resumed his narrative, "we didn't go in. We rang the bell instead."

"And," snorted the superintendent truculently, "the footman said he would enquire if there were any wanted men roaming around waiting to give themselves up."

"And," said Sloan steadily, "we were told that even if Jack the Ripper were loose inside we wouldn't be allowed farther in."

"In the name of the law . . ." began Leeyes weightily.

"Furthermore," reported Sloan unemotionally, "we were also told that should we step inside as unauthorised persons we would be sent to an isolation hospital and kept in strict quarantine until such time as the medical authorities deemed us free of risk to the community."

It was this threat more than the nameless horrors of the Plague that had deterred them.

"And your man?" demanded Leeyes, who never for one moment lost sight of essentials.

"Disappeared."

"Carrying the Lord knows what in the way of germs all over the hospital?"

"We don't know how near the real stuff he got. They said that the next set of doors was locked but they promised to do a big search themselves and tell us if they came up with anything."

"Was there another way out?"

"Yes, sir." Sloan had been a policeman long enough to know that there was always another way out. That went for secure accommodation, too, as often as not. "There's a little staff door at the other end of the laboratories by their changing rooms and . . ." He paused.

"And?" prompted Leeyes urgently. "We haven't got all day, Sloan."

"And they have one of those small service-lift shafts so that—er—items can reach the laboratory without people having to go there in person from other floors."

"Big enough for a man?"

The administrator hadn't thought so for a moment but Sloan knew better. "At a pinch," he said.

"The hospital could be searched. . . ."

"Not without a handful of warrants and a couple of hundred men," said Sloan vigorously. "You should have heard them when I mentioned it. It was about the only thing the matron and the adminstrator agreed about. Except," he added, "that you haven't got to call her matron any more. She's some sort of a nursing officer."

"And as some sort of a police officer," said Leeyes without hesitation, "you shouldn't allow yourself to be bullied by her."

But he said it without his usual panache.

"No, sir."

"The house," said Leeyes. "What did you find there?"

"The insulin bottles," said Sloan. "Five unopened ones that looked all right. One half-empty one that could be all wrong. They've gone straight round to Dr. Dabbe's lab."

"Take out insulin and put in water?" mused Leeyes.

"Simple, when you come to think of it, sir, isn't it?"

"That reminds me, Sloan. What have you done with Crosby?"

* * *

Detective Inspector Sloan had only one thought in his mind when he left the superintendent's office and that was food and drink—well, a cup of tea anyway. The day was slipping by unpunctuated by refreshment for the inner man. There were, he knew, places of work where mealtimes were observed with military precision but the Berebury Police Station was not one of them. Fortunately their canteen staff were as resilient as the rest of them. If their customers wanted food and drink then food and drink would be there for the asking, irrespective of the clock.

And if by any chance a man thought he could eat and then found when faced with food that he couldn't—a common enough situation among men who had their ways among the sad end of society—then nothing was said on either side.

Inspector Harpe's plate was empty.

Sloan sat down beside him. "All quiet on the traffic front, Harry?"

"Just the usual foul-up round the market," he said, pushing his empty plate away. "I've got a friend of yours waiting to see me though."

"Policemen don't have friends," said Sloan. It was one of the things that worried him about his unborn son. Would he get roughed up at school because his father was a copper? He'd have to teach the boy how to handle that early on. . . .

"True." Harpe gave a short laugh. "You'll be pleased to know that Larky Nolson was heard to describe you as a working acquaintance in the pub down by the railway last night."

"So who's the friend?" Some bait Sloan rose to, some he didn't.

"A medico."

"Which particular pillar of the profession?"

"Peter McCavity." Harpe grimaced. "Hardly a pillar."

"More like an unsure foundation," agreed Sloan.

"Come in to confess about yesterday morning's bollard." Harpe jerked his head sourly. "I daresay he's forgotten about Friday's by this time."

"Friday's?" Sloan let his interest in Dr. McCavity's Friday activities show.

"He had the one on the corner of Cranmer Drive on Friday."

"That's leading into Ridley Road, isn't it?"

"There's just the church in between," said Inspector Harpe without conscious irony.

"How do we know?"

"Someone rang in to tell us he'd had it down."

"Who?"

"Ah, they turned shy when we asked them that."

"Pro bono publico?"

"Only up to a point," said Harpe realistically. "An anonymous telephone call isn't evidence."

"Disgusted, Tunbridge Wells, then."

"There was one thing though that was odd, come to think of it."

"Yes?" said Sloan. It was the odd things that made up police work.

"The caller was male."

"Now that is odd," agreed Sloan. Most men who were car drivers had a "There but for the Grace of God . . ." approach to minor motoring matters. Bollards weren't exactly punchballs—but they weren't people either. Not by a long chalk. Bothering to ring in with the driver's car number was usually women's work.

"Shouldn't think the good doctor knows what a no-claims bonus looks like," said Harpe, "so he'll probably . . ."

"When on Friday, Harry?"

Harpe looked up. "Late afternoon, I think. I could check."

"Please."

"Interested?"

"Very."

"Want to come along while he's in?"

"It might help."

It did. In a way. An unexpected way.

Dr. Peter McCavity didn't seem surprised to see Sloan. His lip curled. " 'Cry havoc,' " he declaimed, " 'and let slip the dogs of war.' "

Sloan paused. He didn't go to evening classes like the superintendent but sooner or later all boys' schools performed *Julius Caesar*—if only because it wasn't full of parts for boys who had to pretend to be girls pretending to be boys. Or worse: parts for boys who had to pretend they were girls.

For a moment he searched about in his memory for a suitable rejoinder but all that would come to his mind was something else from another school play. It was a picture of their third-form clown playing Stephano, the drunken butler in *The Tempest*—another play for schoolboys. Prospero's daughter was the only female called for: the competition, as he remembered, had been for the part of Caliban. Stephano had staggered on stage clutching a bottle and saying between hiccups, "Here's my comfort."

Sloan did not say that now.

There was a time and a place for everything.

When he came to think of it, it was the people who did things out of time and out of place who gave them half their trouble down at the police station. The preacher who had written that bit in the Bible about there being a time for everything wasn't wrong. And this wasn't the time for bandying quotations with the doctor. Even if he could think of the right one, which he couldn't.

Inspector Harpe wasn't even attempting to. He was taking down the details of the accident to yesterday's bollard.

"Corner of Eastgate," he said patiently.

" 'The moving finger writes,' " said Dr. McCavity, who had clearly recovered some of his spirits during the course of the morning.

"How about the one you had down on Friday afternoon," said Harpe impassively.

" 'And having writ, moves on,' " said Peter McCavity impenitently.

"Friday," said Harpe. "Junction of Latimer Avenue and Cranmer Drive."

"Another bollard?" said McCavity, faintly tentative.

"So we're told," said Harpe.

"So be it," said Dr. McCavity. Sobered, he was more presentable. He had a rather anxious air of willingness to please about him now.

Sloan stirred. "Near Miss Wansdyke's house."

"Really?" he said without apparent interest. "Yes, I suppose it would be that way. I don't know the house myself."

Sloan maintained silence.

"Dr. Paston always looked after her himself," said McCavity.

"Except when he was away," said Sloan.

McCavity shrugged his shoulders. "I couldn't even sign the cremation certificate, she being my partner's patient. He was ringing round on Monday to find someone outside the practise to complete the second part of the certificate."

"Cremation?" said Sloan. Mortons', the undertakers, had distinctly mentioned burial.

"Didn't you know? She was going to be cremated. It was all laid on. It was what she had wanted and apparently she'd always said so but in the end they didn't take any notice. Nothing's sacred these days, is it?"

* * *

Detective Constable Crosby was still at the Berebury District General Hospital.

His clothes, which lacked credence as a police officer, fitted his new role rather better. He was sitting in the corridor outside Fleming Ward disguised as an anxious relative. This meant that when necessary he was able to sink his head between his hands. Necessity arose only when a nurse who might be Briony Petforth passed.

From this vantage position he could at once observe the door of Sister Fleming's office and the swing doors that gave into the ward. There was another door beyond that of Sister Fleming's office that led he knew not where.

Yet.

Being young and as yet not in possession of any of
Francis Bacon's hostages to Fortune, Crosby wasn't too
familiar with anxiety and how it should be portrayed.
Restlessness came into it, he knew, but too much of
that might draw attention to himself and that was the
last thing he wanted to do. He'd seen people pacing up
and down in hospital corridors too but not with their
heads sunk in their hands, whenever a certain third-
year nurse passed.

So he had settled for an uninviting bench clearly
placed just where it was for those waiting for news from
Fleming Ward. As a situation it was not without interest. Someone came through the swing doors every other
minute and twice they were held open for a patient on a
stretcher coming back to the ward from the operating
theatre. There was, however, no sign of a young man
with auburn hair and freckles wearing a donkey jacket.

For some time he thought perhaps Briony Petforth
wasn't on the ward, and then, soon after the second
stretcher case had arrived, she came through the swing
doors and made straight for Sister Fleming's office.
Seconds later the sister sallied forth in person and went
through into the ward with Nurse Petforth. Moments
after that an invisible loudspeaker started paging the
duty house officer.

Crosby was so wrapped up in this living charade that
he didn't even notice at first when a large woman approached. He gave a genuine start when she suddenly
plumped down on the bench beside him.

"Sorry, lad," she said, "but there's only one bus I can
catch in from Cullingoak to be at the hospital when visiting starts and I might as well wait here as at the bus
station."

He nodded and turned his attention back to the ward
doors. As any television producer could have told him,
it was compulsive viewing.

"Got someone in here, too, have you?" enquired the
woman presently.

"Er—yes," he said, collecting himself.

A harassed-looking young man in a white coat with a
stethoscope dangling from his pocket had just turned
onto Fleming Ward. He would be the house surgeon.

"It's my husband," she said gratuitously. "Hasn't been well all summer and in the end they said they'd better operate."

"Bad luck," said Crosby.

"What's yours in with?"

Crsoby cast about swiftly in his mind. He had an aunt who had had to go into hospital once. "Gallstones," he said with conviction.

The fat woman patted his arm. For one awful moment Crosby was seized with sudden doubt, and he began to wonder if gallstones were a peculiarly feminine complaint. Then she said kindly, "That's not serious, dear, these days, is it?"

"With complications," said the detective constable a little coldly, his confidence restored. No hospital visitor likes to be demonstrated as visiting someone less ill than the next person's relative: even when it is not so much a case of *malade imaginaire* as of imaginary invalid.

"Ah, that's different," she said at once. The fat woman began to rearrange her parcels. "My hubby now—they said in the beginning that he wasn't going to be straightforward."

It was Detective Constable Crosby's turn to sound sympathetic. He hoped that it wasn't the stout woman's husband who was causing all the commotion on the ward. Yet another doctor had now appeared and a bottle of blood had been rushed through the swing doors by someone else. There was no sign though of anyone resembling Nicholas Petforth.

The fat woman was speaking again.

"Pardon?" he said.

"The person you've come to see," she said patiently.

"Yes?" Warily.

"Has he been in here long? Perhaps my hubby's in the next bed."

"Not long," said Crosby truthfully, adding even more accurately, "I'm not sure exactly where he is."

She nodded comfortably. "They do move them about so."

"Or even," said Crosby, artistically painting in a finer touch, "if he'll really want to see me."

This struck an immediate chord with his neighbour. "You never can tell how hospital will take people, can you?"

"No," he said. What he was actually doing was considering whether the door beyond Sister Fleming's office led to the sluice or not.

"Perhaps he'll have them to show you," she remarked.

"What?"

"In a bottle."

"Show me what in a bottle?" demanded Crosby wildly.

"His gallstones."

Crosby's aunt had spared him this.

"They give them to you sometimes," she said knowledgeably.

"Souvenirs?" said the constable weakly. After all they had a Black Museum at New Scotland Yard as incongruous, didn't they?

"They did my next-door neighbour," said the woman, "when she had hers done."

"Did they?" said Crosby, discovering like many another inventor before him that those who build Kafkaesque castles in the air run the risk of the whole tottering edifice that they have fabricated brick by unsteady brick crumbling at the first touch of reality.

"Seven as big as marbles," the fat woman said.

The swing doors of the ward opened suddenly and Sister Fleming appeared. She made for her own office. If she noticed those sitting on the corridor bench she gave no sign of it. Like the rest of the hospital staff, she seemed to have the gift of ignoring those who waited on benches—or perhaps it was a skill honed down to a fine art. Just to be on the safe side, though, Crosby tucked his feet well out of sight. It wasn't so much that they were large: just that they were a policeman's feet.

Then another loudspeaker call went out. The senior surgical registrar was wanted on Fleming Ward.

Now.

"If not sooner," muttered Crosby to himself. He reckoned he was as good as the next man at reading between those sorts of lines.

Sister surged back onto the ward.

The fat lady began to rearrange her parcels again.

Crosby decided that this was his moment.

"Just going along the corridor," he murmured with absolute truth.

All Sister Fleming's forces were deployed on the ward and no one even looked at him as he slipped past the door of her office. He could hear noises from a kitchen somewhere but it was the door beyond Sister Fleming's office that he was making for. If anyone had an eye on a rendezvous with Nurse Briony Petforth or was in search of a quiet place to hide, this was the ideal spot for it.

Crosby advanced cautiously. On closer examination he decided it wasn't the sluice. That he could now see—and hear—was beyond. He opened the door. He was in a linen storeroom of some description. Racks of sheets were faintly visible. He stepped forward and began to feel for the light switch.

It was the last thing he remembered.

Something very heavy came down behind his neck and hit him hard. A vicious reverberating explosion took place inside the confines of his skull. Detective Constable Crosby subsided in a kaleidoscope of mental colour and for a long time knew no more.

Chapter 12

Alkali, tartar, salt in preparation,
Matters combust or in coagulation.

Detective Inspector Sloan had had to take another constable with him from the Berebury Police Station instead of Detective Constable Crosby. He didn't want to interview Dr. John Paston alone. Actually he didn't really want to take the time to interview Dr. Paston at all at this particular moment. Not with Nicholas Petforth at large and the whole case a tangle of loose ends but there was in him ingrained an early training married to a dogged persistence which allowed no opening in an investigation to go unexplored.

The general practitioner's manner towards the two policemen could not have been described as inviting. He sat quite motionless behind his desk waiting for Sloan to speak.

"I have come," began that officer without preamble, "about the late Miss Beatrice Wansdyke."

"Again?" said the doctor.

"And," continued Sloan, "about your pecuniary interest in her death."

Dr. Paston gave a short laugh. "Oh, that!"

"That," said Sloan totally unimpressed. In his time he had heard a great many dubious actions dismissed with a short laugh by the people who had perpetrated them. The activities had ranged from minor peccadillo to major misdemeanour but long ago he had come to realise that the enormity of crime lay—like beauty—solely in the eye of the beholder. The eye of the person who had committed it was always firmly glued to the wrong end of a telescope. The victim's eye view was usually more accurate.

"Rather a grand way of describing a small legacy, isn't it?" remarked Dr. Paston.

"Were you or were you not," Sloan forged on with his inquisition, "aware of it at the time of her death?"

"No." He hesitated for a moment and then said, "No, as a matter of fact I wasn't."

"Let me go back to Monday when she was found."

"Yes?"

"You were informed of her death."

"Indeed I was."

"And visited the house."

"That is so."

"And began to prepare a cremation certificate."

"Yes." He looked puzzled. "Why?"

"Beatrice had always told me that that was what she wanted."

"So," asked Sloan, "why are Mortons' now preparing for burial?"

"That was the family," said the general practitioner immediately. From his tone it was obvious that families were an everyday complication of general practise.

"Which part of the family?" enquired Sloan cautiously. One thing he had learned over the years was that families did not invariably present themselves as united groups.

"It was George Wansdyke who actually mentioned it to me," said Paston, "but knowing the set-up there I daresay it was Pauline Wansdyke who didn't like the idea."

"Ah."

"The Hartley-Powells," Dr. Paston informed him drily, "are all buried over in East Calleshire."

"I see."

"In the ancient village churchyard at Great Rooden."

"And always have been?"

"Since the Norman Conquest," said Paston gravely. "At least."

"Some people find ancestor worship easier with tombstones."

"I'd even begun to lay on a colleague," amplified the doctor, "to sign the second part of the cremation certificate when George Wansdyke told me the family wanted a burial instead."

"And when did you hear about the legacy?"

"In the same breath as the burial." He tightened his lips into the semblance of a smile. "Wansdyke's a businessman, not a sentimentalist, you know."

Sloan, no time waster himself, nodded.

"At least," said Paston, "he did read over the message that came with the bequest."

" 'In small recognition of his unfailing kindness over many years,' " quoted Sloan from his notes.

For the first time the general practitioner looked momentarily disconcerted. "She wasn't the sort of woman to leave everything to a home for lost dogs."

"No," said Sloan consideringly. Not for one moment had he forgotten a dead Airedale either. Late dog. Like late pig. Now that was from somewhere very far down in his subconscious. "You had no idea it was going to happen?"

"None," he said vigorously. "And if I may say so, Inspector, I should have signed a declaration to that effect on the cremation certificate without hesitation."

"Quite so," said Sloan quietly. "Were you surprised?"

"That, of course, is something quite different." He hesitated and considered this. "No, not inordinately."

"Have you any plans for using the money?" Suddenly Sloan felt self-conscious. He must sound as silly as a cub reporter talking to the winner of a football pool. The answer he got, though, wasn't exactly what he expected.

"The nuts," said the doctor astringently, "come when the teeth have gone."

"Pardon?"

"Let me put it like this, Inspector." The general practitioner drew breath. "I do not for one moment anticipate that exactly one sixteenth of Beatrice Wansdyke's estate is going to alter my entire way of life."

"I see, sir." Now who was it had drummed into Sloan's head that your income was the only thing you could anticipate: and that most of the other uses of the word were incorrect? His English master perhaps. He'd been taught mathematics too. . . . "You did say a sixteenth, Doctor, didn't you?"

"My partner is entitled to half of anything I inherit from a patient."

"I didn't know that," said Sloan quite spontaneously.

"Every contingency," said the general practitioner ironically, "is provided for in a medical partnership agreement."

"Even down to splitting legacies?"

"That is quite a normal feature," said Paston drily. "Even millionaires bleed."

"Quite so." Detective Inspector Sloan started to do a spot of quick calculating.

"Millionaires don't crop up often," said the doctor.

"But when they do . . ."

"There isn't an unseemly stampede in the practise to attend them." He coughed. "If you come to think about it, Inspector, I'm sure you'll see . . ."

Sloan did come to think about it.

Dr. Paston might be able to maintain a rather lofty attitude to money and riotous loving. His junior partner, though, was quite a different matter. It was quite obvious to all and sundry that young Dr. Peter McCavity had an instant use for every liquid asset that he could lay his hands on.

* * *

"I may only be a forensic pathologist," said a plaintive voice down Sloan's telephone, "but even I can distinguish margarine from butter."

"I beg your pardon, Doctor?"

The detective inspector had come back to his desk at the police station in Berebury to find a heap of messages piled on it. He had been riffling through them when the telephone had rung and Dr. Dabbe had been put through to him.

He turned the message sheets over with his free hand.

The superintendnt wanted a progress report.

He would.

Inspector Harpe of Traffic Division would like him to drop by his department. Happy Harry—he was always known as Happy Harry because he had never been seen to smile—was far too cautious to say why on paper.

Very well. He, Sloan, would drop by Traffic Division.

Soonest: as they said in telegrams.

Mrs. Margaret Sloan had telephoned to say that she was going out shopping during the afternoon. That was why there would be no reply if he should happen to ring home.

He looked at his watch and felt a stab of guilt. He was uneasy about the phrasing too. He didn't like the way the message had been put. "Should happen to ring" carried overtones. Of course he would have rung as soon as he could. . . .

The last message was from the duty officer in the control room. He wished Detective Inspector Sloan to know that there had been no answer to calls to Detective Constable Crosby on his personal radio. They had been trying to raise him over the air from the control room for the best part of half an hour. Would he have gone out of receiving range without notifying them?

And did Detective Inspector Sloan want anything done about it?

Sloan replaced the messages on his desk.

"Margarine from butter," repeated Dr. Dabbe into his ear over the telephone.

"What?" said Sloan blankly. Now he would have to down tools and find out what Crosby had got up to.

"And water from insulin," continued the pathologist. "Even I can spot the difference."

"Er—good," said Sloan.

"And it was water, old chap."

Sloan concentrated his mind on what the pathologist was saying, banishing with a great effort the possible import of each of the messages waiting for him.

"No doubt about it," said Dr. Dabbe.

"Someone had been at her insulin." All right, then. At least they knew where they were now.

"Someone," said Dabbe, "had removed it from the bottle and substituted water."

"So"—Sloan worked out his conclusions aloud as he went along—"she'd been having no insulin at all since she began to use that particular bottle. . . ."

"Correct."

"And she'd . . ." He stopped and gave their subject the dignity of a name. "Miss Wansdyke had been giving herself injections of water instead of insulin."

"That," agreed Dr. Dabbe with caution, "would account for her symptoms certainly." The pathologist spent a lot of his working life in the law courts and the long experience had made its mark.

"And . . ."

"There was something else that could be inferred as well."

"Was there?"

"So I checked."

"And?"

"I wasn't wrong."

"Well?"

"The water that was still left in the insulin bottle was quite sterile."

"Oh," said Sloan blankly.

"If it hadn't been," explained the doctor kindly, "she would probably have had a nasty abscess at the injection site by the time she died."

"Ah," said Sloan in quite a different tone. "And she'd have gone back to her general practitioner with that, wouldn't she?"

"She would. Painful things, abscesses."

"Someone might have put two and two together then."

"They might." The pathologist wasn't making any promises in that quarter.

"I see." Sloan nodded. "I should have thought of that, shouldn't I?" Time was when he'd never even seen that sort of thing—an abscess at an injection site. That was before the abuse of drugs became a feature of police life. Though there seemed a world of difference between youngsters dying in filthy holes and corners and a middle-aged schoolmistress meticulously treating her diabetes, presumably an unsterile injection had the same effect on all members of the human race. If you prick us, do we not bleed . . . no, that was something different.

"Someone took care," remarked the pathologist.

"The other bottles . . ."

"Right as rain," said Dabbe with singular inappropriateness.

"But there had been insulin in the one she was using though, hadn't there? Once, I mean."

"Oh, yes. It started off as the real stuff because there's still a very faint trace of it in the water left in the bottle."

"The bottle labelled insulin," said Sloan heavily, thinking of someone ill and failing, increasing her dose and not getting any better. "Nasty."

"Murder always is," said Dabbe. "And I should know."

"Doctor . . ."

"Yes?"

"Let me get this straight. Miss Wansdyke had been using this duff bottle up until the time she died. Agreed?"

"Agreed."

"And all the other bottles are perfectly all right?"

"Agreed."

"So," said Sloan, "if she had happened to pick on one of the other bottles in the batch she was using then she wouldn't have died when she did?"

"No."

Sloan paused. Then:

"Are you saying, Doctor," he asked, thinking aloud, "that someone must have tampered with the current one after she started using it? Not before?"

"Oh, yes," returned Dabbe promptly. "You see, Sloan, the only—er—nondestructive way into and out of that sort of bottle is by using a hypodermic syringe and pushing the needle through the rubber composition cap."

"Ah, I see . . ."

"The patient might very well have noticed a puncture hole in a new bottle that she hadn't used before."

"And would have suspected something then," concurred Sloan.

"The dirty deed," pronounced Dr. Dabbe in the manner of a pantomime king, "will turn out to have been done after she started using that particular bottle. You'll see."

"So," said Sloan, who had always been quick at school, "if we could work out how many doses she had out of it we could expect to find an extra hole in the rubber cap?"

"We could," said the pathologist. "It would be clever stuff all right but . . ."

"But?"

"Too clever for open court."

"Ah." They—policeman and pathologist both—knew the dangers that lay in that direction. The defence could be as clever as it liked. That pleased everyone except the police. The prosecution had to be more careful about the weight of evidence. Pitching the full resources of the establishment against the lonely figure in the dock had a counterproductive effect on some juries. Especially nowadays.

"Juries don't like it," said Dabbe.

"Juries," said Sloan shortly, "aren't what they used to be."

"Twelve good men and true."

"That's as may be," said Sloan. Since the property qualification had gone, juries were a random selection. Very. And it showed in the verdicts they brought in. "You don't know where you are with juries these days. Take obscenity, for instance."

"Anything to oblige," murmured Dabbe negligently.

"Often as not your new-style jury doesn't even know what the prosecution is going on about."

"Need French lessons, do they?"

"And when it is explained to them," said Sloan stiffly, "they won't convict. Can't see what all the fuss is about."

"I can tell you anyway," complained Dabbe, "that too clever by half prosecutions don't go down well either, and as for . . ."

"The trouble is"—Sloan rarely let himself be carried

away in this fashion—"that they can't be flattered into thinking they understand any more. They know there are a lot of things they can't grasp. People have been telling them so all their lives."

"They all know though," agreed Dabbe sagely, "when they're being buttered up."

"And they take against expert witnesses," said Sloan, not entirely inconsequentially.

"There's nothing new about that," said the pathologist sturdily. "A water-tight case isn't water-tight if the jury doesn't like it."

Sloan agreed. As he did so his eye was caught by the little heap of message sheets on his desk. He came back to the matter in hand.

"I think we can agree then," he said, "that it wasn't chance that Miss Wansdyke was using this doctored bottle now."

"If you're asking my opinion," said Dabbe, "I should say on the contrary. By the way, Sloan . . ."

"Yes?"

"Could you be a bit more careful with your adjectives? Gives the profession a bad name. Doctored, indeed! Whatever next?"

*   *   *

The very ill patient on Fleming Ward did die.

In spite of all that the doctors and modern medical science could do, the last enemy—death—supervened. Nature, as is her wont, won in the end. As it happened the patient wasn't the husband of the stout countrywoman to whom Detective Constable Crosby had been speaking earlier but he had been somebody's husband and Sister Fleming's first duty was to tell his wife that he had died. Where handkerchief work was involved, so to speak, she always felt the task to be hers. When she delegated it to the young house officers she usually had to see the relative herself all over again.

Once more with feeling, in fact.

On Fleming Ward itself a certain briskness set in as the man died. Death represented a new procession of tasks and another course of action. It was a clear-cut and speedy course. Porters were summoned, screens appeared. The house surgeon and a registrar, suddenly idle, were treated to a little oblique and educative propaganda from the ward sister *en passant.*

"I'll fight for a patient for all I'm worth," said Sister Fleming quite fiercely, "but once they've gone I forget them completely."

The two young doctors got the message and melted away, consoled, to other duties.

The ward sister always had been one to improve the shining hour. She turned her attention to the nurses.

"And when you've made up a fresh bed, Nurse Petforth," she said sharply, "be sure to check the drip on the hemicolectomy over there."

"Yes, Sister," said Briony obediently. In prison, in the army, in the police force, you might be a name and number: in a hospital it was quite different. If you were a patient on a medical ward you were known by the disease you had. If you were on a surgical ward it was by the name of the operation you had been admitted to have.

"That drip should have been attended to before," she said.

"Yes, Sister."

"And nurse . . ." She turned her baleful gaze towards the probationer who was helping Briony Petforth with her bedmaking and whose very first encounter with death this had been.

"Yes, Sister," said the young nurse tremulously.

"You should have noticed before now that the appendix has come round from his anaesthetic."

"Yes, Sister."

"See to him," she commanded, "as soon as you've finished the bed."

Rightly calculating that righteous indignation at this cavalier approach to the Pale Horseman of the Apocalypse would banish any backward thoughts about the patient thay had just lost, Sister Fleming swept off to see the ward clerk about the admissions waiting list.

Acknowledged tartar Sister Fleming might be, but there were times when she came into her own.

"The patient is dead, long live the patient," muttered

Briony rebelliously, attacking the bedmaking with a certain savagery. While the dirty linen was being swept into a bag by the other hurse she set off for the linen room to collect fresh sheets and pillow cases.

Something—she didn't know what—was stopping her opening the door properly. She gave it an extra push and stepped inside, feeling for the light switch. It was then that she saw the crumpled figure of a man lying supine on the floor.

Where another girl might have screamed, Briony Petforth reminded herself that she was a nurse. She bent down cautiously, noticing as she did so the blood coming from a wound on the back of the man's head.

She thought she recognised the man's face but it wasn't his name that she used.

"Oh, Nick . . ." she moaned. "Oh, Nick . . ."

Chapter 13

We seek and seek, and were it once discovered
We should be safe enough—expenses covered.

"What!" exploded Leeyes. "They've found who? Attacked? And injured, did you say?"

"Detective Constable Crosby."

"Where?" spluttered Leeyes. "Wait until I . . ."

"In the hospital, sir. On Fleming Ward."

"We should have searched it," declared Leeyes inevitably.

Sloan ploughed on with the meagre information at hand. The superintendent was a great one for being wise after the event. "Crosby was found lying on the floor in the linen room, sir."

"Assaulted in the execution of his duty," intoned Leeyes in tone suitable for a memorial service.

"He's unconscious," Sloan informed him hastily. "Not dead."

"One of my men," said Leeyes sonorously.

"They've taken him down to Casualty."

"A good man, Crosby."

"Er . . . quite," said Sloan, savouring the occasion. Superintendent Leeyes's geese were only swans now and then.

"We'll get whoever did this, Sloan," he said militantly, "if we don't do anything else. And soon."

"Yes, of course," said Sloan calmly. It was a fact of police life that people who killed or tried to kill policemen were usually caught sooner or later. Sooner, more often than not. For some reason too arcane for an ordinary person to explore, those who attacked policemen in Great Britain ran out of support from friends and relatives earlier than other wrong-doers did. And more commonly than with most transgressors someone turned them in. Perhaps as a penalty for breaking the rules by which the game of cops and robbers was played? Sloan didn't know.

"If they so much as touch a hair of his head," growled Leeyes, "I'll . . ."

"They've hit it," announced Sloan badly. "Quite hard. Already." The superintendent's press conference would come later. He could say whatever he liked at that. Clichés and all. Now was a time for facts.

"Grievous bodily harm then," responded Leeyes automatically.

"Could be," admitted Sloan. "He hasn't come round yet. I'm on my way over there now."

"That's right," said Leeyes obscurely. "Close the ranks."

"We've put out a general alert."

"Good, good. No one else missing, is there?" At times like this all of the superintendent's flock were dear to him.

"No," said Sloan, startled. "Crosby and I are the only two on this job anyway."

"Better write your own report out then before you leave," said Leeyes lugubriously, "in case anything happens to you too."

"He's only a boy really," said Sloan, heroically suppressing a number of other tempting retorts to this last. "If in fact it was actually Nicholas Petforth who hit Crosby."

"Boys," pronounced Leeyes with feeling, "can cause more trouble then men."

"It may not have been him, of course," said Sloan fairly. "There's another possibility. All Briony Petforth will say is that she opened the door of the linen room and found Crosby there."

"Ah."

"She also insists, sir, that she hasn't seen her brother since before their aunt died."

"He would always know where to find her though, Sloan."

"I gather," said Sloan drily, "that he is in the habit of coming up on the ward when he wants something."

"Money?"

"Probably. She didn't say."

"I shouldn't be surprised," said the superintendent, who, was, after all, in a better position to judge than most men.

Sloan, momentarily diverted, voiced something that had been puzzling him all along. "I've been thinking, sir, that Beatrice Wansdyke's money must have come from somewhere pretty out of the ordinary."

Superintendent Leeyes snorted gently but did not speak.

"She didn't inherit it," pursued Sloan, "or win it on the pools, nothing's been stolen that we don't know about, the bank isn't unhappy about where it came from . . ."

"If it wasn't for the fact that someone had it in for her over the insulin and the dog," said Leeyes judiciously, "I'd have said the answer was easy."

"Sir?"

"Computer error, Sloan. I had a gas bill once . . ."

"This other possibility on the ward," said Sloan, who had heard about the gas bill before, "is something we've got to think about."

"What's that?"

"I am told that a frequent visitor on the men's surgical ward," said Sloan, "is Inspector Harpe's favourite medical motorist."

"Dr. McCavity?"

"He was a house officer at the hospital before he went into general practise with Dr. Paston," Sloan informed him. "Got quite friendly with Nurse Petforth while he was about it."

"Ah," said Leeyes alertly. The superintendent had never been able to make up his mind if sex was a more powerful ingredient of crime than money. He was, however, willing to consider the proposition at any time.

"But she wasn't having any."

"Like that, was it," grunted Leeyes.

"Turned him down."

"It happens all the time."

"In favour," pressed on Sloan, "of young Dr. Elspin."

"You won't remember this, Sloan."

"Sir?"

"Before your time."

Sloan steeled himself to silence. Every so often some hapless soul at the police station had—metaphorically, at least—to splash his way ashore at Walcheren alongside the superintendent in a wartime landing craft, rifle at the ready.

"There was this radio programme, Sloan, called ITMA."

Sloan breathed again. It wasn't going to be Walcheren.

"They had a character sketch about a young Dr. Hardcastle," said the superintendent reminiscently. "Ivy used to say he was lovely. . . ."

"Being turned down," said Sloan as repressively as he dared, "doesn't seem to have deterred Dr. McCavity."

"He didn't get the message?"

"This last couple of weeks he's been more persistent than usual. Sister Fleming's turned him out of the ward several times even though he's a doctor."

The superintendent stopped thinking about wartime radio comedy programmes. "Are you saying that he might have thought he was onto something?"

"I am merely pointing out," said Sloan astringently, "that his ardour seems to have enjoyed a bit of a comeback recently."

"Love and lolly?" said Leeyes, contemplating this.

"As Dr. Paston's partner he collects a sixteenth of the deceased's estate. . . ."

Leeyes nodded.

"As Briony Petforth's husband . . ."

"A clear way to another eighth," said the superintendent practically. The repeal of the Married Women's Property Act had no more signified with him than with most husbands. "You'd better look into that."

Sloan didn't write his report before he went to the Berebury District General Hospital to see Crosby, but he did telephone his own home.

There was no reply.

* * *

Detective Constable Crosby had come around by the time Sloan reached the Accident and Emergency Department of the Berebury Hospital.

His first words uttered on regaining consciousness had not been notably helpful.

"He just complained about his head," reported Sister Casualty.

Sloan nodded.

"I'm not surprised really," said the sister. "You should see the knock he's had."

Sloan was resigned. "I expect that I'll have to."

"I don't know what he hit me with," complained the patient bitterly. He was lying in an examination cubicle looking surprisingly cherubic in hospital pyjamas. Every now and then he ran an exploratory finger near the back of his head where he had been hit, found afresh that it hurt and took it away again.

"They haven't found a weapon yet," said Sloan.

"Try looking for a sledge hammer," groaned Crosby.

There might well be a Noble Army of Martyrs but quite clearly Detective Constable Crosby of the Berebury Police Force had no intention of being numbered among them.

"He has got quite a contusion there," said the sister fairly. "The doctor's going to look at it in a minute."

Crosby groaned again. "Bury me at Wounded Knee."

"This man who hit you . . ." began Sloan.

"The blighter must have been holed up in that linen room all the time."

"I suppose," said Sloan, "he was waiting for a chance to talk to his sister. If it was Petforth."

"I don't know what he was going to do," Crosby reminded him with a certain savagery, "but what he actually did was to hit me. Hard."

"It's not too serious," said Sister Casualty with professional briskness.

"It's not your head," said Crosby plaintively.

"The man who hit you," repeated Sloan, who had professional obligations too, "did you see him?"

Crosby brought his hand up to the back of his head again. "This is where he hit me. Here." He accidentally touched the spot. "Ouch . . ."

"I've already told you not to . . ." began the sister.

"He got me from behind," insisted Crosby. "That's why I never saw a thing. Except stars," he added mordantly.

"He was waiting in there all right," said Sloan. "He'd been sitting on a pile of blankets."

"Saving his strength," said the victim. "All I can say is that for someone who'd gone native he packed a pretty punch."

"Opted out of society," said Sloan. "That's what he'd done." The real natives of this sceptr'd isle lived in semidetached houses and watched television in the evenings.

"If you ask me," said a disgruntled Crosby, "he'd been practising with a pile driver while he was up on the motorway site. . . ."

Suddenly the curtain of the cubicle in Casualty was twitched back and a very young-looking man in a white coat approached.

Crosby started nervously.

Sloan was near enough to read the taped identification label on his breast pocket. It said "Junior House Surgeon."

"I've just come to put a few stitches in your scalp," he announced cheerfully.

Crosby obviously regarded the cheerfulness as misplaced.

"It *is* Mr. Crosby, isn't it?" enquired the doctor.

All men are equal in hospital.

Or nearly.

"It is," said Crosby in doom-laden tones.

Like steam giving way to sail, Detective Inspector Sloan yielded in the name of the law to the ancient profession of healing.

"I'll be getting along then, Crosby," he said, moving away.

Crosby was still taking in the doctor's appearance. He looked a real infant beside the well-built policeman. He had long wavy hair and sported an amulet with distinctly pagan overtones. He was also trying to grow a beard.

"It won't take a minute," said the young doctor heartily.

Crosby rolled his eyes and muttered something under his breath.

Sister Casualty showed Detective Inspector Sloan out.

"I've noticed the policemen are getting younger too," she said obliquely, walking with him to the door of the department. "And, Inspector . . ."

"Sister?"

"The house surgeon's mother does know he's out."

"Pardon? What was that?"

"Constable Crosby wondered if she knew."

* * *

"Of course I don't know what a policeman was doing in the ward linen cupboard," retorted the distraught girl. "And neither does my cousin, George. Do you?"

"No," said Dr. Roger Elspin.

"All I know," said Briony Petforth helplessly, "is that he was there and that I found him and . . ." Her voice trailed away.

"And?" prompted Elspin.

"And that if anything else is going to happen after all this, in spite of what you say, Roger, I don't think that I can . . ."

He interrupted her with, "You've had quite a week, darling, haven't you?"

Her manner changed abruptly. "Oh, Roger . . ."

"What with one thing and another," he said largely. Nearly two years of working in a hospital had taught him the value of unspecific statements that sounded comforting. And of the great importance of always sounding sympathetic. Being bracing made enemies of patients faster than the most painful treatment.

"First poor Aunt Beatrice," she said.

"And now this," he said for her.

"Nothing makes sense any more." She pushed her hair back under her cap. "Why should there be policemen in the hospital at all?"

The obstetrics registrar shook his head. "I don't know."

"And why wasn't Dr. Paston's death certificate for Aunt Beatrice good enough in the first place? Tell me that."

"I don't know." He frowned. "We only had one lecture on jurisprudence when I was a student. It's not enough really."

She shuddered. "Post-mortems are all very well but only when it's someone you don't know."

"That goes for a lot of things," he said soberly.

"I suppose it does." She sighed. "Like illness."

"Like childbirth," said the obstetrics registrar meaningfully.

"Oh, Roger . . ."

"I think we'd better adopt."

"Oh, no, we won't," she said hotly.

"Or do without the patter of tiny feet then and stay childless."

"I don't know about you," she said strenuously, "but I'm proposing to have six babies in quick succession." Her face clouded again. "I don't agree with small families."

"No."

She looked at him. "Roger, you're taking on quite a bit, aren't you?"

"If by that you mean your brother Nick . . ."

"He's a big worry especially if . . ." She fell silent.

"He's old enough to take care of himself, you know," said Roger Elspin.

"I only wish he was," said Nick Petforth's sister practically.

"He's certainly in a spot of trouble if he biffed that young copper."

"I thought he was dead at first," she shuddered. "Now are you sure you want to marry into our family?"

"Quite sure," he said calmly.

"The police wanted to know if Nick had a key to Aunt Beatrice's house."

"Had he?"

"We all had."

"We?"

"Nick, George, and me. Aunt always said we were welcome any time, even if she was out. She was out a lot, you know. She liked to spend her spare time down at the firm's lab working on this theory of hers."

"Turning air into gold."

"It was our home, after all," said Briony, ignoring this, "and anyway she never knew when she might be ill. She was very sensible, you know. Isolde would only attack a stranger so it was all right for us to have keys." She caught her breath. "Roger, I don't understand about Isolde. . . ."

"No. Did the police ask anything else?"

"They wanted to know if Peter McCavity had been up to the ward again. Sister must have told them about that."

"And had he?" asked Elspin quickly.

"Oh, he's always around these days."

"Bothering you?" Elspin's colour deepened.

She shook her head listlessly. "Not bothering exactly. Just around." She looked across at the registrar. "By the way, Roger, someone told me that they'd seen you up on Fleming this afternoon."

He nodded. "I was."

"You were?"

"I came up to snatch a quick kiss between deliveries."

"Oh, I see." She essayed a smile. "It would have had to come out of your ration today."

"I needed a pick-me-up, nurse. It's been a busy day on the maternity unit."

"I didn't see you."

"You had a bit of a flap on," he reminded her.

"That's right." She looked at him, wide-eyed. "Do

you know I'd almost forgotten about that already? And I would never have thought I could so soon. Terrifying, isn't it?"

"That's life."

"He was such a nice man, too, the patient who died."

Dr. Roger Elspin shot a quick glance at his watch. "Talking of patients reminds me that I should have a head coming up to crowning by now."

* * *

"Someone," pronounced Inspector Harpe of Traffic Division, "made darn sure that we linked Dr. Peter McCavity up with that smashed bollard near Ridley Road on Friday afternoon."

"And a man it was to boot," murmured Sloan. "Not a woman." That had been the curious thing. It was the curious things which added up in a case.

"So," said Harpe, "we ran a paint test."

"The good old exchange principle," said the detective inspector.

"We shouldn't get far without it up in this department," said the traffic man.

What Isaac Newton and gravity were to physics so the exchange principle was to police work. Fundamental. Objects could never meet without exchanging something of each other. Never. (Well, hardly ever.) And that usually went for human beings who touched—let alone things that went bump in the night too.

"Paint of car left on bollard?" guessed Sloan. Being a policeman and not a philosopher, he liked to leave the general for the particular as soon as he could.

"Better than that."

"Bit of bollard still attached to car? Oh, well done, Harry!"

Inspector Harpe permitted himself a rare grin of triumph. "Embedded in the headlight."

"McCavity's had another bollard, though, since Friday's, hasn't he?" asked Sloan.

The traffic inspector was unperturbed. Quite clever defence lawyers had been trying to catch him out for years. On oath.

"No, Sloan. The second bollard was yellow. The Friday one was white."

"That helps."

"What I want to know," said Happy Harry, "is whether you want me to run any other sort of test on the man rather than on the vehicle."

Sloan considered this. "He's certainly going to lose his licence one of these days anyway, isn't he?"

"Unless," said Inspector Harpe sourly, "whoever brings him in doesn't play the procedure game properly."

"It's a lot better than it was, Harry," said Sloan, answering the thought rather than the words. Breathalysers had been progress indeed.

"The Leith police dismisseth us," lisped the traffic man mockingly.

"My client," responded Sloan in courtroom tones, "has always had a speech impediment."

"He fell off a chalk line drawn on the floor of the police station."

"My client has a wooden leg. Surely the officer noticed?"

"He couldn't focus."

"An artificial eye."

"Drowsy . . ."

"Tired."

"He attempted to embrace a desk."

"Deeply shocked."

"He was quite unable to complete Rhomberg's test and touch the tip of his nose with his finger while his eyes were shut."

"The officer completely misinterpreted his gesture."

"He was pathologically talkative."

"My client always recites *The Boy Stood on the Burning Deck* when under stress."

"He complained that little green men were running round the charge room."

"Come, come, Officer," declaimed Sloan histrionically, "you must know my client's reputation as a humourist."

Happy Harry grunted and brought the surrealistic word picture to an end. "It's all very well for you to joke, Sloan. Let me tell you that the first man I put the finger on for driving under the influence—he was as drunk as a monkey's uncle—actually fell into the road when I opened the driver's door. . . ."

"And got off?"

"Not a stain on his character. Taught me a lot, did that."

"Has Dr. McCavity any blots on the escutcheon already?"

"Two."

Sloan was not surprised.

"And he's heading for a third," said Inspector Harpe, adding the quaintly old-fashioned phrase, "unless he mends his ways."

Sloan nodded. What the young doctor's resting blood alcohol level was, so to speak, didn't bear thinking about. "Leave it for today, Harry, though," he said, falling back on a police cliché. "There may be graver charges."

Inspector Harpe lifted an eyebrow. "Like that, is it?"

"Too soon to say."

"There have been other medical murderers, of course," mused Harpe.

"You don't need to tell me. The superintendent keeps on about them too."

"Harley Crippen," said Harpe immediately.

"Everyone always says him first."

"Bert Ruxton."

"Nasty piece of work."

"There was a poisoner, too, wasn't there?" said Harpe.

"And how," said Sloan inelegantly. "William Palmer." Madame de Brinvilliers might be *hors concours* as a poisoner but Dr. William Palmer had done his best to keep up. "Palmer the Poisoner, that was."

"That the lot?"

"No, it isn't," said Sloan briskly. "There was Dr. Lamson, who killed his brother-in-law for gain, and Dr. Pritchard, who poisoned his wife."

"Cream," said Harpe suddenly. "Neil Cream. He was a doctor, too, wasn't he?"

"So was Marcel Petiot," said Sloan. "He said he'd killed sixty-three people."

"They've had the training, of course," said Harpe. "By the way, we've had a request for a bobby at Wansdyke and Darnley's for Friday."

"This Friday?"

"They've got some sort of new product shindig on," said the traffic man. "Thought you might be interested. Their works being down near the bridge makes the parking a bit of a problem."

"I wish my problems were only parking ones," said Sloan fervently.

"Good Lord, yes," said Harpe. "I'd forgotten that bit about all your troubles being little ones. How are things?"

Sloan looked at him with dawning horror as he realised that he, too, had momentarily forgotten all about his wife and the unborn baby.

And in favour of murder.

"Fine, fine," he said hastily.

Chapter 14

*For all our cunning, when all's tried and done
That stone won't yield itself to anyone.*

"There is one thing," pronounced Superintendent Leeyes heavily, "that doesn't make sense."

"Sir?" As far as Sloan was concerned there were a lot of things about the death of Beatrice Gwendoline Wansdyke which didn't make sense.

"We still don't know for certain that any of these people really expect anything more than peanuts from Beatrice Wansdyke's estate."

Sloan sighed. There would be no mileage, he knew, in reminding the superintendent that as a motive for murder peanuts were good enough any day of the week. Dotty as it might seem, traditionally the stakes did not have to be as high for murder as they usually were for burglary.

"Not one of them," persisted Leeyes, "has given us the tiniest clue that they know they're in the big-money league."

"Someone hit Crosby."

"People are always hitting policemen," said Leeyes largely. "It's an occupational hazard."

"Someone changed insulin for water."

Leeyes accepted this without contradiction. "Ah, that's different. I grant you that, Sloan."

"It means that the malice was well aforethought," said Sloan. That was something he'd been thinking about quite a lot. The planning. This murder had been well contrived.

"I can see that without the missing insulin there

would be no case to answer," agreed Leeyes, submerging the assault on Constable Crosby's person without a backward thought.

"There isn't exactly a case," Sloan reminded him. "Not yet, anyway. But there will be."

"Up boys and at 'em," murmured Leeyes absently.

"I have been checking on one or two points with the bank, though, sir."

"A clammy lot, bankers."

"There were one or two crumbs they were prepared to let me have."

"Well?"

"They gave me the cut-off dates of their current account statement cycle."

"You could have worked that out for yourself."

"Perhaps," remarked Sloan philosophically, "that's why they disclosed them."

"Big deal."

"And, quite unofficially mind you, we've established the exact date the big money reached Beatrice Wansdyke's account."

"You have, have you?"

"Her bank statements were in the bureau in her sitting room."

"So it wasn't beyond Crosby."

"No." Sloan coughed. "When we tackled the bank again after that they did reveal—saw no harm in letting us know—that the large sum we were—er—interested in was received as one lump payment."

"Some lump."

"Some chicken, some neck," agreed Sloan, adding, "perhaps that's why it attracted attention."

"Nonsense," said Leeyes robustly. "A hundredth part of that sort of lump going into my current account would positively startle the manager."

"Yes, sir." The Sloan family income was modest, too. Police incomes were.

"And when exactly did Miss Wansdyke hit the jackpot?"

"I'll give you one guess," said Sloan.

"Sloan," said Leeyes testily, "are you trying to tell me something?"

"That payment didn't appear on her last bank statement, sir."

"So it's come in since the cut-off date?"

"The day after," said Sloan. "That's when it arrived."

"So it would be how long before she got her next statement?"

"A calendar month."

"Do you mean to say that if for any reason she didn't know about the money it would be the best part of four weeks before she would find out?"

"Unless she went in to the bank to ask what her current account stood at."

Superintendent Leeyes considered this. "Is what you are getting at, Sloan, the idea that she might not have known it was there?"

"All we know is that it wasn't on her last bank statement because we've looked at that. And," Sloan added judiciously, "that she hadn't gone in for being one of the last of the big spenders since it arrived."

"How did you work that out?"

"Crosby again, sir," he said, giving credit where credit was due. "Her cheque book was in the same drawer."

"He might make a detective if he lives long enough."

"Somebody," said Sloan flatly, "tried to see that he didn't."

Leeyes grunted.

"At least," said Sloan, "it explains the Ridley Road life-style. I should say that up until last month she had a Ridley Road income to match."

"The bank," rumbled Leeyes. "Surely they'd have told her that it had arrived."

"They say that they hadn't notified her of its arrival because they had been instructed that no notification was required."

"And they," said Superintendent Leeyes cynically, "always obey the last order too, do they? Who do they think they are? The army?"

"They obey instructions," said Sloan a little wearily. "They don't make decisions." He often wondered if those whose only duty was to carry out instructions ever realised how well off they were.

Leeyes snorted. "In our way of business you have to do both."

"Yes, sir."

"That's what sorts out the men from the boys."

"Yes, sir." There was no absolution to be had from blind obedience to orders in the police line of duty. Sloan knew that well enough. But all the same there was still always hell to pay if you broke the rules and followed your own nose and it didn't work.

And sometimes even if it did.

"If it wasn't for the insulin being tampered with," said Sloan fervently, "I'd have said the money was there by mistake."

"Get anything else out of the bank?" enquired Leeyes.

"Only that the Wansdyke family had banked there for three generations. They didn't seem to mind telling me that."

"That's not information," said Leeyes gratuitously. "That's advertising."

* * *

"No, Inspector," repeated George Wansdyke with some firmness, "I have not seen Nicholas Petforth since my aunt died." He did not sound regretful. "We put an obituary notice in the newspaper and hoped he would see that, though I believe he keeps in touch with his sister, Briony, from time to time."

The businessman was sitting at his desk in his office at the works of Wansdyke and Darnley. At the other side of the same desk, moving restlessly from foot to foot, was Bill Benfleet, the public relations man who had also been there earlier in the day. Wansdyke pushed the piece of paper they had both been studying into Benfleet's hands saying, "Some other time, Bill. . . ."

Benfleet shook his head. "Sorry, Mr. Wansdyke, but no."

"Look, Bill, this really will have to wait for a bit."

"It won't wait," said Benfleet flatly.

"It'll have to," said Wansdyke more than a little briskly. He indicated Sloan. "Can't you see that, man?"

The public relations man stood his ground. "It won't wait any longer. Not if you want it for Friday."

"Of course we want it for Friday," snapped a goaded Wansdyke. "That's the whole point."

"Then"—Bill Benfleet was adamant—"it's got to be done now."

"But . . ."

"I've got my girl staying on to type this tonight," said Benfleet with the air of one unanswerably clinching his argument. "Late."

Detective Inspector Sloan found it in his heart to be sorry for any man caught between the Scylla of his employer and the Charybdis of his secretary.

Wansdyke, too, must have seen the force of what Benfleet was saying. He ran his hand through his hair and capitulated. "You'll just have to do it yourself then, Bill."

"I can't," explained Benfleet patiently. "I've told you before I don't know enough about the product."

Sloan turned his head with Wimbledon-like interest to see how George Wansdyke would take that particular ball.

"Your public relations people don't usually let a little thing like that stand in your way," said Wansdyke with an attempt at lightness.

"I'm an advertising man," Benfleet came back with a straight volley. "Not an industrial chemist."

"Then ask one of them"—irritably.

"Nobody seems to know enough about it to say the right things."

"I'll grant you that," said Wansdyke more gracefully. "It's Mr. Darnley's pigeon really."

"And he's somewhere over the Atlantic," said Benfleet. "I hope."

"So do I. All right, Bill. I'll do it just as soon as the inspector's gone."

Sloan came in as on cue. "We're just checking really, sir."

"Sorry about all that," said Wansdyke as Bill Ben-

fleet withdrew at last. "Friday's the day for a new product launching and we're just tying up one or two loose
ends."

"So am I," said Sloan simply.

"What—er—oh, yes, of course, Inspector. What can
I do for you now?"

"You can tell me a little more about Petforth."

"Nicholas? There's not a lot to tell you. Typical of
his generation, I suppose. Never settled to anything. No
money. Not particularly good at school. My aunt always said he had brains and she should know but he
never used them that I know of."

Sloan didn't trouble to write down what he was saying. "Did he ever want to come into your firm?"

Wansdyke gave a short laugh. "And do some real
work? Never, Inspector. He prefers to live by sponging
on his sister and his aunt."

Sloan said nothing. The motorway site hadn't
sounded like a cushy job to him.

"Beatrice always had a soft spot for him, whatever
he did," said George Wansdyke.

"She's proved that, hasn't she, sir?"

"What? How do you work that out?"

"She left him half her worldly goods, didn't she, sir?"

"Oh, her will. Yes, of course. I was forgetting that."

"Does he know about it?"

"Not from me," said Wansdyke. "I don't know
where he is."

"From his sister?"

"Possibly." Wansdyke shrugged his shoulders.

"From his aunt herself, maybe?"

"Perhaps," said Wansdyke. "She might have told
him."

"She didn't tell you she had?"

"No," said Wansdyke. "Beatrice only told me that I
was her sole executor."

"So Petforth might have known for some time that
he was going to inherit?"

"Maybe." Wansdyke pulled his lips down. "Not that
half of Beatrice's estate will keep him in comfort for the
rest of his days and I suspect that that's the sort of support he's looking for."

Sloan said, "Aren't we all, sir?"

Wansdyke looked up sharply.

"Your new product, sir, that you're launching on Friday."

George Wansdyke smiled thinly. "You win, Inspector. Of course we're hoping that will do the same for us. I must say comfort for the rest of our days would suit us all here at Wansdyke and Darnley very well."

"How near did Miss Wansdyke get to having a press release of her own?"

"I don't really know, Inspector. My partner, Malcolm Darnley, is the technical one—I'm responsible for the business side of things—so I couldn't say for certain how far she'd got. He'd know. They used to chat a lot."

"She spent a lot of time down here?"

"Oh, yes, indeed. It was a fascinating quest for a chemist."

"Something from nothing," said Sloan appositely.

"I think she found it a relaxation after a week's teaching," said the other man.

"She would have made notes."

Wansdyke's face relaxed into a rueful grin. "Inspector, all research chemists make notes. Hundreds and hundreds of them. Filing them, I assure you, is a nightmare."

"Where would they be, sir?"

"Beatrice's notes? At her home, I should think. They're not here."

"Perhaps, sir," he said, "you'd let me know if you come across them." Detective Constable Crosby hadn't found them there but Sloan did not say so. They'd be searching the house in Ridley Road again anyway now that they knew about the insulin not being insulin, so to speak.

"Of course, Inspector." Wansdyke frowned. "Naturally, if you want them."

"Then," said Sloan courteously, "I won't come between you and your press release any more."

* * *

It was the best meal he had eaten for days. Detective Inspector Sloan said as much to his wife as he set his knife and fork down.

She smiled and murmured, "We both had too much."

"Couldn't very well waste anything as good as that, could we?" he said comfortably. "It wouldn't be right."

"It'll be the other sort of waist we'll have to watch soon, won't we?" said Margaret Sloan. "The one that needs a tape measure."

"Fulfilled has two meanings, too," he said, settling into his own fireside chair, "seeing as we're playing with words."

She fetched coffee and poured out two cups.

Presently she asked, "Went the day well?"

Over the years of married congress the two of them had devised an unwritten formula for the policeman's wife's equivalent of the business executive's wife's routine enquiry "Had a good day at the office, dear?" Margaret Sloan never put the question until she had seen to his bodily comfort. She always left out the verbal endearment too. There were other—better—ways of expressing that. . . .

And to her eternal credit she never pursued a negative response.

Today, though, she got a full answer.

"Crosby caught a packet." Her husband told her all about the attack on the young constable's person.

She shuddered. "Poor boy."

"We think it may have been Nick Petforth."

"The nephew?"

"He was around at the time. We do know that." Propinquity came into crime no matter what the moralists said, else why pray to be delivered from temptation?

"Around where?" asked his wife, settling down her coffee cup.

"Fleming Ward."

She frowned in recollection. "That's where the niece works, isn't it? The one I overheard talking to Dr. Elspin."

"It is."

Margaret Sloan stared into the fire and said, "It's

like a horrible mixture of two parlour games. Both jumbled up together . . ."

"Two?" Sloan looked up quizzically. He'd never been much of a man for parlour games. Not of that sort, anyway.

"Murder," she said. "Surely you remember playing that?"

"In the dark," he assured her.

"And . . ." Her voice trailed away.

"And?"

"And"—she didn't even like saying it—"Happy Families."

She got an unexpectedly earnest answer.

"It's in families that there's the greatest danger of murder," he said seriously. Nervous old ladies, afraid to go out in the dark, never believed it, of course. Nobody liked to believe that the greatest danger of murder came from one's nearest and dearest; that home was where the real danger of violence lay. The bedroom for the woman, the kitchen for the man, and the bathroom for the baby—where they were most likely to be strangled, stabbed, and drowned—in that order. The Home Office did their sums and said so.

"Miss Bun, the baker's daughter, and all that," she murmured.

"I thought for a moment," he admitted, "that you were going to say the other game was Consequences."

"I'd forgotten that one."

"It's the one that nobody bent ever plays," he said quickly. "If they did and sat down and worked out all the consequences of what they were doing there wouldn't be any crime and I'd be out of work. . . ." This inability to see the consequences of malefaction was what marked out your criminal.

But not your murderer.

Sloan knew that too.

Your murderer murdered to bring about consequences that were desirable to him.

Which was quite different.

"And Crosby?" asked his wife. "How is he now?"

A slow grin came over Sloan's face. "Better than Humpty Dumpty."

"And all the King's horses . . ." she began.

"And all the King's men—if that's what you call the National Health Service."

"Have put him together again?"

"Well, a young house surgeon was going to have a try. So young that Crosby was affronted."

"Poor boy," said Margaret Sloan again. Ambiguously.

"They're keeping him in hospital, though, tonight, to be on the safe side." His mind still on his own excellent meal, Sloan said, "He won't have eaten as well as this in there."

"No."

Something in the dryness of her tone made him look up, his face crinkling into a smile. "I'll smuggle you something in to the maternity ward, love," he promised, "in a paper bag under Sister Fleming's nose."

"You'll be too busy chasing villains to come to see me," she said mischievously.

"You wait," he said. "I'll be like those natives who camp at the bottom of the bed."

"You haven't seen the ward sister," said Margaret Sloan.

"Not friendly to natives?"

She smiled the rather remote smile of the heavily pregnant. "More coffee?"

"We never found a ransom note for the dog," he said, passing his cup. "I forgot to tell the super that. We did look in the house, just in case."

"You may be sitting in your own home, Detective Inspector Sloan," she observed, "but you haven't really left off working, have you?"

"It's all this nourishment," he said. "My brain is responding to it."

"Coffee coming up." She frowned. "So someone killed the dog for another reason?"

"To stir her up, perhaps. Dr. Dabbe did say a missing dog could upset someone in her state quite a bit, if they were attached to it."

"If Miss Wansdyke wasn't well for any reason," said Margaret Sloan intuitively, "could the dog have given the alarm? It was an Airedale, wasn't it?"

"If it's all the same with you," said her husband, "I'll stick to a St. Bernard when I'm lost in the snow. They've had the practise. You can send one of those with the brandy in that little keg round its neck."

"In the sort of places where you're likely to get lost," she came back smartly, "a working ferret would probably find you quicker."

"That's right—bite the hand that feeds you."

"I like that, Dennis Sloan." She started to struggle out of her chair. "Just you wait until I get my figure back."

"Not in your condition, please," he begged. "Don't do anything rash."

"Rash!"

"The dog," he said, hastily reverting to the late Beatrice Wansdyke, "might have barked if it couldn't get out of the house after she got really ill."

"Except that it was already dead." Margaret Sloan subsided into her chair again. "I wish I didn't feel so much like a stranded whale."

"Or if someone came to the house." He regarded her affectionately across the hearth. "It won't be for long now, love. . . ."

"The Airedale would have barked then," agreed his wife, adding fervently, "The sooner, the better."

"I was thinking," said Sloan, "that it also might have been killed in case if and when anyone called at the house and the dog didn't bark. . . ."

"You've been reading Sherlock Holmes again."

". . . in the night."

"I thought *The Hound of the Baskervilles* was going to come into this," she said, reaching for her knitting.

"Bound to," agreed Sloan gravely.

"I can knit and listen. . . ."

"If the dog didn't bark when someone called . . ."

"Because it wasn't there to bark."

"Whoever called would assume that Beatrice Wansdyke was out."

"And go away again," she said.

"While all the time she was lying there getting more and more ill."

"Poor thing," said Margaret Sloan compassionately.

"You come along to court when the time comes and remind them of that," said her husband. "Usually by the time defence counsel has said his piece on behalf of the murderer everyone's forgotten all about the victim. . . ."

By the time the following dawn had broken Detective Inspector Sloan had forgotten all about the victim too.

For the time being.

Hours later a tiny tug at his shoulder woke him from deep, carefree sleep.

"Have you got indigestion?" enquired a voice in the region of his left ear.

"No," he said sleepily.

"I have."

"Best meal I've had in days," he murmured dreamily.

"I think I ate too much."

"I'm sure I did. And very nice too." He grunted. "What time is it?"

"Two o'clock."

He promptly turned and buried his face in the pillow.

"If it isn't indigestion," said the same voice tightly, "then I think it's the baby starting."

Chapter 15

It's made us squander all we ever had,
Losses enough to drive us mad.

It is a fact universally acknowledged by all experienced policemen that babies, which come in all shapes, sizes, and colours, arrive in only two ways: before reaching the hospital and after reaching the hospital. In the nature of things it is only the first alternative that finds its way into both the occurrence book at the police station and the private nightmares of the officer concerned. It was naturally also the one which weighed on Detective Inspector Sloan's mind as he dressed with speed and backed his car out of the garage with unusual haste (and at considerable danger to the lawn mower).

"If it comes on the way," he joked between lips that had gone unexpectedly dry, "you'll have to christen him after me anyway."

A rather abstracted smile was all he got by way of answer to that.

"It's the done thing," he insisted. Rumour—unconfirmed rumour, it is true—even had it that somewhere down in the town of Berebury was a youth (otherwise to Fame unknown) who as a lusty and precipitate infant had been named after Superintendent Leeyes. Even superintendents, it was conceded down at the station, must have been constables once.

"Have you got my suitcase?" asked his wife more practically.

"In the boot," said Sloan. "Come on. . . ."

"Your supper's in the larder."

158

"Supper?" he said, momentarily bewildered. "It's the middle of the night. . . ."

"You'll be hungry by suppertime," she forecast. "It's on the middle shelf."

"Do come on."

"Unless you're going to go over to your mother's, of course."

"Margaret Sloan," he said firmly, "are you coming out to the car or aren't you?" This was no time to be talking of mothers-in-law.

"Have you locked the back door?"

"I have."

"Well, what are we waiting for then?" she asked with feminine perversity.

Sloan clamped his lips together.

She was sitting beside him in the car before she said suddenly, "The cat!"

"Out," snapped Sloan.

"I only asked."

"Sorry, love." The cat had had its kittens one night in the spring in the garden shed unbeknown to all until after the happy event. Sloan felt a swift upsurge of admiration of the animal kingdom.

Once put on the main road, he stepped up the speed of the car, sparing an anxious glance to his left from time to time. He started to search around in his mind for something comforting to say . . . the right phrase for the moment. . . .

"I forgot to leave a note for the milkman," she murmured before he could think of the *mot juste*.

"Just asses' milk from tomorrow?" he said, caught off guard.

"You'll only need one pint."

"I propose drinking nothing but pink champagne tomorrow."

"It may be a boy."

"Blue champagne, then."

"Fool," she said affectionately.

"Asses' milk," he said. "I was right the first time."

He negotiated two bends in the road and then drew up as a lonely set of traffic lights showed red. There seemed something faintly idiotic about their stationary car standing at a halt in solitary splendour in front of a red light in the middle of the night. He shot a quick glance at his wife. She seemed all right.

"If the Martians landed now," he said, "they'd have a job working out human behaviour—us sitting here like this without anybody about until the yellow light shows up."

"Until the green light shows up," she said. "I'm not having Harry Harpe pinning anything on you tonight. His boys will be about somewhere. They always are."

At right angles to the traffic signals for motorists were the pedestrian ones, the forbidding red man dimmed, the permissive green one glowing.

"I wonder what the Martians would make of the little green man over there," he said.

"Jack-in-the-Green," she said absently.

"What?"

"The Green Man. The pagan touch."

"Oh, yes, of course." Their little Red Book of advice on having babies had been strong on humouring.

"Maypoles, and all that," she said enigmatically.

The red light gave way to amber and then green while the little green man facing pedestrians was succeeded by the red one. The red man reminded Sloan of the devil but he didn't say so. It didn't seem to be the right moment to mention the Prince of Darkness. He set off down the road again at a more decorous pace than hitherto. The urgency of his journey had given way to a thought even more terrifying than that of birth on the way to the hospital.

False alarm?

Their way led down a hill towards the deserted town centre. The hospital was the other side of that. The road went past the police station, its blue light the only sign of wakefulness in sight.

"I spy blue," said Margaret Sloan. It had been how she greeted him when they were first engaged.

"I spy black," chanted Sloan.

"I spy a copper with a . . ." She caught her breath suddenly and broke off in mid-speech, bending forwards. He couldn't see her face.

He took his left hand off the steering wheel and put

it over her white knuckles. And he put his right foot on the accelerator.

"Sorry." She took a deep breath and then said, "I'm all right now."

"It won't take long to get there this time of night."

"And at this rate," she said shakily.

He slowed down.

But only for a moment.

* * *

If there is one type of suspect which all the police forces the world over find less difficult in tracking down than any other it is the escapee with nowhere to go. Foxes have holes and birds of the air have nests but with the hearths of home and family well and truly stopped a man on the run is a vulnerable man.

Detective Inspector Sloan found that expectant fathers were similarly without anywhere immediate to go. The journey to the Berebury District General Hospital duly accomplished and the sanctuary of the maternity ward achieved at last, Sloan himself was now at something of a loose end.

At the door of the ward it had been quite kindly suggested to him that he go away and have a cup of tea for half an hour or so. As there had been no information about where he could procure such a commodity in the middle of the night Sloan rightly interpreted this as telling him he wasn't wanted for a little while.

He decided as a first step to park his car.

He steered it around to the visitors' car park, switched off the ignition, and made himself think about that other soul with nowhere to go—Nicholas Petforth. This required quite an effort as his whole inclination was to let his thoughts dwell exclusively on Margaret Sloan. Nicholas Petforth had to all intents and purposes disappeared as surely as if he had been touched by a conjurer's wand. He had not returned to the house of squatters in Luston, he had not been near the motorway site beyond the Calleford Road, he had not been back to Fleming Ward.

Sloan was quite sure of this last.

Detective Constable Crosby had been admitted to the

ward with a bandage on his head and a personal radio in his pyjama pocket. And though the girl herself didn't know it another policeman was keeping a watchful eye on Briony Petforth in the nurses' home. Nick Petforth, though, concluded Sloan, must be somewhere. And as it was by no means a warm night that somewhere was probably under cover. By October even a fugitive from justice needed a roof over his head during the hours of darkness.

Sloan looked at his watch: another twenty-five minutes before he could go back to the ward.

He wound the window of the driver's door down and sniffed the night air. It was distinctly chilly. Not that he was contemplating going for a walk. No policeman who had once done his years on the beat ever voluntarily put one foot in front of the other again except in the line of duty. Sloan had done his share of two and a half miles to the hour, fourteen miles to the day, in his time. More than his share probably, or did everyone always think that?

"And," his old sergeant had said grittily to him on his first day, "if you come back saying you're dead beat I'll run you out of town."

So he hadn't.

He'd finished his first foot patrol and reported instead that as days went it had taken a lot of beating. . . .

A raw constable learned a lot from his first sergeant.

Like the importance of finding out where to get a cup of tea any hour of the night or day.

"Unless you're a good kitchen range-finder, my lad," Sloan could hear him saying even now, his first sergeant, "you'll never make a good copper because you'll always be thirsty. And that's a bad thing."

Sloan wound the window of his car up again and started the engine. He was a pretty poor policeman if he couldn't find a cup of tea somewhere. He turned out of the car park and headed for the town centre again. The blue lamp of the law was still shining above the police station doorway.

The night duty officer greeted him ironically. "We never close."

More importantly neither did the canteen.

A couple of Inspector Harpe's night duty traffic patrol having their rest break nodded to him without curiosity. They knew that the Criminal Investigation Department worked at night too. The phrase "ungodly hours" was no mere slip of the tongue. . . .

Sloan settled himself down in a corner of the canteen with a cup of tea. There was one thing to be said for being here at the police station in the middle of the night as opposed to the middle of the day. Superintendent Leeyes was not usually around in the night on the lookout for fools not to suffer gladly. For some reason the notion of fools set up another train of thought in Sloan's mind. He hoped that they weren't being fools in the case of Beatrice Gwendoline Wansdyke.

The neat elderly spinster and her dog who had inhabited the neat ordinary house in Ridley Road seemed very far removed from exotic sums of money. And yet the neat elderly spinster and her dog were both dead and the neat ordinary house empty. . . .

Sloan set his cup down.

The neat ordinary house was empty.

He pushed his tea cup away and got to his feet. There was just time for him to slip round to Ridley Road before he went back to the hospital and check.

It might not be empty.

* * *

Mrs. Margaret Sloan had her cup of tea brought to her bedside. She was in a nightdress now and lying back in bed.

"More comfortable now are you, dear?" she was asked.

"Yes, thank you." Her face was quite flushed all the same.

"How's the pain?"

"Not too bad." Her concentrated expression belied the words.

The midwife nodded. "We'll give you something for it."

Nonverbal communication ranked high in hospitals. Heightened colour never went unnoticed either.

"Thank you." She caught her breath. "That would help."

"Just relax as much as you can."

Margaret Sloan managed a short derisive laugh.

"I know, dear," said the nurse patiently, "but do try to save your strength all the same. You're going to need it later." She straightened the bedclothes with an automatic twitch in the true Florence Nightingale tradition and went on, "You could probably get a little sleep, too, you know, if you put your mind to it."

"Sleep!" echoed the patient in patent disbelief.

The midwife was too wise to argue. She changed the subject instead. "Your husband'll be back presently."

"I don't know about that," said Mrs. Margaret Sloan. "He's a policeman."

* * *

Detective Inspector Sloan's car was the only one about in Ridley Road, Berebury. He stopped well short of Miss Wansdyke's house and let himself quietly out of his car. He padded noiselessly along the pavement and went straight past the house, noting what he could without turning his head. Save that the window curtains were undrawn, it looked just as did the neighbouring houses. The only immediate difference that sprang to the eye was that there were no empty milk bottles outside the door.

Milk bottles reminded him of home.

And duty.

He took a quick look at his luminous watch. He mustn't be too long about this. He was due back at the hospital pretty promptly. He turned when he got to the end of the road and walked back towards number fifty-nine. The gate did not creak and he was standing outside the front door in a moment.

He still had a key.

So, he reminded himself, did a number of other people.

The lock slid back easily and he was soon inside the

hall. He shone his torch very briefly to get his bearings. He went swiftly through the downstairs rooms first. He wasn't going to have anyone hitting him from behind. That had been a lesson learned a long time ago. He flashed his torch quickly over the kitchen sink and draining board. Traces of human occupation showed up there more often than anywhere else. That had been another lesson learned.

Both sink and draining board here were quite bare. So either there was no one in the house or else they were being very careful indeed. Admittedly the place had the feel of desertion. His torch swept over a dog's food bowl near the stove. Nobody had moved that away yet. Not, he conceded at once, that there had been a lot of time for any tidying up to be done. George Wansdyke, sole executor, had a big business to run, especially with his partner away. An aunt's affairs would have to take their turn.

Sloan moved out of the kitchen and back through the hall. He would take a quick look round upstairs and then get back to the hospital. He put his hand on the newel post and felt with his foot for the first step.

"Don't come any further," said a voice from the top of the stairs.

Chapter 16

Go where they may a man can always tell
Such people by their pungent brimstone smell.

"How is the pain now, dear?" the midwife enquired of Mrs. Margarent Sloan.

There was a significant pause before she could speak. Then she managed to say, "Not too good."

The midwife nodded with the briskness of one not in pain and at once brought into play a piece of equipment which was standing beside the bed. "Take a deep breath of this," she commanded, "when you feel a pain coming on."

Mrs. Sloan reached out hungrily for the proffered mask. Plunging her face deeply into it, she sucked the anaesthetic gas and air mixture with avidity.

"That better?" asked the nurse encouragingly.

She nodded, still clutching the face mask.

When the pain had passed she removed it and asked, "Is my husband back yet?"

"Not yet," said the midwife, adding with uncanny— but quite unwitting—prescience, "I expect he's been held up somewhere."

* * *

Detective Inspector Sloan, father-to-be, swung back to the side of the stairs and out of the direct line of whoever was above. He transferred his torch to his left hand, keeping his right free. The voice had been a youngish one. He decided to provoke it into speech

166

again. He tapped the side of the banister rail with the handle of his torch.

"Don't move," said the voice at once.

Sloan did move. Noisily.

"Don't move, I said," came the voice again. Less assuredly this time.

Sloan stepped around in front of the staircase again. There was a certain amount of thin light coming from an uncurtained window near the landing at the top of the stairs. When he got around far enough to see up in that direction though he was disappointed. All he could make out was a shape standing in a position of vantage at the head of the stairs.

He paused for thought.

There was no chance of rushing someone standing eight feet above ground level. He knew that. Especially with stairs wide enough for only one person at a time. Builders of mediaeval castles had known what they were about when they designed their tiny turret staircases inside their towers. One man with a sword standing at the top of one of these could keep an army at bay. Besides, he, Christopher Dennis Sloan, Detective Inspector, who should know better, had committed the cardinal sin of coming here alone, and without leaving word of what he was about.

So if he failed there would be bureaucratic trouble. Going it alone was countenanced in the police force only when married to success. Hunches could be played by police officers all right—but they had to be winning hunches.

Or else.

Very cautiously he advanced and put his foot on the bottom step of the staircase.

It creaked.

It would.

The figure at the top of the stairs promptly took a step downwards. Sloan could see now that the man's right hand had something in it. It could have been a poker. He decided on a change of tactics.

"Suppose," said Sloan amiably, "you tell me your name."

This arrested the descent.

"Suppose," countered the voice at the top of the stairs, "you tell me yours."

"Police," said Sloan.

A short laugh came from above. "I thought it was either cops or robbers and the silver's not worth stealing."

"Your name," said Sloan again. The superintendent was a great believer in maintaining the initiative and it rubbed off.

"Legion," said the voice promptly.

"I think," said Sloan quietly, "that it's Nicholas Petforth."

"And if it is?" challenged the voice.

"Then we've been looking for you."

"We seek him here," came mockingly out of the darkness, "we seek him there."

"You're wanted for questioning," said Sloan more prosaically.

"I didn't think it was for a dog licence."

"No," said Sloan, "it wasn't." The beginnings of an idea had come to him.

"Coming for me at the squat and then hounding me at work."

"The hospital," Sloan reminded him. In the dim light he was trying to count the number of stairs.

"There, too," said the voice with a distinct note of grievance.

"You led us a real dance halfway round the hospital."

"I've probably caught the dreaded lurgies all because of you."

"That's why you went up to Fleming Ward afterwards to see your sister, isn't it?" He thought there were eleven steps in the staircase.

"She's a nurse," mumbled the voice. "I thought she'd know."

"Got any symptoms yet?" enquired Sloan heartlessly. With sybilline cunning he put his foot on the second stair up from the hall at the same moment as he spoke.

"No."

"Not gone green all over or anything like that, have

you?" The great thing now, decided Sloan, was to maintain the dialogue.

"No," said the figure at the top of the stairs, "and I'm not going to turn into a toad either just for Malcolm Darnley's benefit."

"Come again?" said Sloan. Maintaining a dialogue with the man above wasn't as difficult as it might have been: but it was unexpected.

"Malcolm Darnley," said the voice above richly, "has set up a group to help toads across this new motorway."

"It's in their way, too, is it?" said Sloan unsurprised. He felt for the third step with his foot.

"Cuts right across their patch."

"Pity, that." Sloan was really taking a second look at the landing window. If he attempted to advance in an upright position he would be silhouetted against what little light there was. There would have to be a better way up. He dropped to his knees. The stair he was on creaked as he did so.

"Don't come any further," said the voice hoarsely.

"If," said Sloan with the utmost cordiality, "you're not going to turn into a toad what about being a prince?"

"A prince?" The remark seemed to have caught its hearer off balance.

"Seems as if it's always one or the other," said Sloan, "in all the best fairy stories." He was working his way up the stairs on his knees now. Like the pilgrims did when they climbed the Penitential Steps in the Vatican in Rome.

"Not even to please a fairy princess," replied the voice. Its owner sounded really quite young.

Sloan had to keep silent now. Speech would have betrayed how near to his quarry he was. In fact his only problem was how to keep his breathing under control: it had to be soundless.

"Besides," said the voice, "I think I'd rather be a toad."

As Detective Inspector Sloan tensed himself in preparation for a grab at the ankles of the man standing above he remembered something else about toads: that there was a variety of the species called the midwife toad.

It lent a lot of power to his elbow.

* * *

In a different place and for a different reason someone else had also been trying hard to control her breathing.

Trying harder.

Or perhaps it's just more difficult.

"Don't hold your breath," adjured the midwife.

Mrs. Sloan thought briefly about a suitable retort but didn't make it.

Breath was too precious now to be wasted on words.

Besides, words were magnificently irrelevant.

True she was making a sound of some sort but in a way altogether disassociated from what she was actually thinking. It might have been coming from someone else so little control had she over it.

"And remember to rest in between pains," continued the person in charge in an admonitory manner.

Being in charge, decided Margaret Sloan to herself in a detached fashion, was an illusion. Anyone who thought they were in control of events in a delivery ward was living in cloud cuckoo-land. Events were in control of everyone else. An event, anyway. She took a breath of shuddering proportions, and decided that anyone who wasn't the mother or the baby at a confinement was only on the touchline.

Not part of the real action at all.

It was a moment or two before she realised that her immediate world now consisted of more than herself, the midwife, and a gas and air machine. Aware that someone else was standing beside her bed, she turned her head with an effort and consciously tried to focus her gaze on the figure.

Detective Inspector Sloan moistened his lips uneasily. "Sorry I'm a bit late. . . ."

Any husband to any wife.

"Where have you been?" she asked.

Any wife to any husband, as the poet said.

Chapter 17

*What about merchants? Lord! They don't
    maintain
A fixed prosperity, believe you me.*

He did set out to tell her where he'd been.

"Nick Petforth's safely in a cell now," he said.

He couldn't tell if she was listening to him or not.

"And a bit worse for wear, I must say."

Or even if she wanted to hear.

"The station sergeant," he plunged on, "didn't like the look of him at all when I took him in."

He had begun by patting her hand, then holding it.

"I told him that he'd fallen down a flight of stairs in the course of arrest, which was true in a manner of speaking."

Margaret Sloan's eyes were closed. He couldn't tell what she was thinking.

"And he said," Sloan told her, "that he'd heard that one before and I could tell it to the marines if I wanted to but that the court wouldn't like it."

Margaret Sloan made no response but she left her hand in his.

Sloan carried gallantly on. "He asked me what I was charging him with. Hitting Crosby, I said. Do you know what he said to that?"

The hand that lay in his tightened but still Margaret Sloan did not speak.

"No?" Sloan grinned. "You won't believe this, Margaret, but he sighed deeply—the station sergeant of all people and you know how strait-laced he is—he sighed and said, 'Inspector Sloan, you don't know how I envy

him. Hitting Crosby is something I've wanted to do myself for a long time.' "

Had there been a faint twitch at the edge of Margaret Sloan's lips or had he imagined it?

"Almost worth going on a charge for, he said it
would have been."

Margaret Sloan said nothing.

"I know the feeling," said Sloan more to himself than
to her.

After that, Sloan, too, fell silent and presently the
hand that held his slackened its tension and dropped
away.

"She's asleep," pronounced a figure in blue over his
shoulder. "We gave her something. You can go away
again for a little while. Not too long, mind."

*   *   *

Sloan looked at his watch. Morning was breaking
and the hospital was coming to life again for a new day.
He would go to Fleming Ward and visit someone else.

Detective Constable Crosby, tousled hair extruding
between layers of bandage, struggled to sit up as Sloan
approached his bed. "Morning, sir."

"How went the night?"

"No sign of Nick Petforth," said Crosby, "and his
sister went off duty at suppertime."

"He's in a cell," said Sloan.

"Ah." Crosby sank back on his pillows.

"But I don't think he did more than hit you."

"That's enough, isn't it?" demanded the victim, immediately aggrieved. "It hurt."

Sloan looked at the detective constable's bandaged
head with a new dispassion. A spell in the delivery
room of the maternity ward altered a man's outlook on
pain.

"Besides," said the patient, "I didn't get a wink of
sleep last night."

"He's admitted hitting you and denied everything
else," said Sloan succinctly.

"You can't sleep in a place like this even without a

headache," said Crosby, preoccupied as any other invalid with his own state of health.

Sloan wondered what Superintendent Leeyes would have said to that, and then to his surprise heard himself saying it aloud. He must be getting old. "I don't know what the force is coming to."

"Petforth's got the best motive," said Crosby, reluctantly abandoning the role of valetudinarian.

"The biggest, you mean," said Sloan.

"Half the deceased's estate." Crosby thought for a moment. "And he'd got the means, too, hadn't he, sir?"

"Had he?" asked Sloan.

"If there weren't half a dozen hypodermic syringes sculling around that squat I'll eat my hat."

Sloan nodded. He could believe that half of that lot were on those sorts of drugs.

"And," insisted Crosby, "he'd got the opportunity. Ah, good . . ." His face brightened. "There's the tea trolley. I thought they were never coming with it."

"By opportunity," continued Sloan, smiling winningly at the nurse in charge of the teapot, "I suppose you mean that he had a key to Beatrice Wansdyke's house?"

"I do." Crosby grimaced. "The tea's even worse here than at the station."

"Never."

"Got bicarbonate of soda in it, I expect."

"Whatever for?" said Sloan, startled. He didn't want to be done good to by any hospital so early in the day.

"To make it look darker and go further, of course."

Sloan's mother had never stooped to such tactics. He promptly went off the tea.

Crosby leant back against his pillows with the air of one winding up a case. "There you are, sir. Motive, means, and opportunity—what more do you want?"

"Proof," said Sloan: but it wasn't what he meant.

"Ah." Crosby smoothed down the sheet.

"No," said Sloan, immediately amending what he had said, "that's not true. What I really want to know is exactly where all that money came from and what it was doing sitting in the account of the late Miss B. G.

Wansdyke. . . ." He paused. Somewhere at the back of his mind then something had rung a little bell. He searched his memory but Mnemosyne, daughter of Heaven, mother of the Muses, sat back and answer came there none. "And, Crosby," he added in the absence of elucidation, "I want to know exactly what the hurry was."

"What hurry?" asked Crosby, lending a nice touch of verisimilitude to his remark by lying back negligently in his bed, ostentatiously remote from the pace of life at the police station.

"The hurry about her dying when she did." Sloan regarded the constable straightly: a hospital cut a man off from the world so. "We'll have to get you out of here, Crosby, before the rot sets in."

"I can't see why it was an against-the-clock job, sir."

"I can," said Sloan briskly. "You see, if by any chance it wasn't her money and she didn't know about it either . . ."

"If," said Crosby.

"Then she stood to find out about it pretty soon, didn't she?"

"How?"

"When she got her next bank statement, of course. That hit on your head didn't damage your brain, did it?"

"And," said Crosby with dignity, "the bank statements are due out again at the end of this week."

"Or the beginning of next. You can never be sure with a computer."

"More tea?" enquired a new voice.

"What's that? Oh, no, thank you, nurse. . . . I must be going soon," said Sloan, withdrawing his cup.

"Suppose, though," advanced Crosby cautiously, "she had got her bank statement or happened to enquire about the balance at the bank?"

"Keep supposing," said Sloan. "Suppose for the sake of argument she's an honest woman." Usually, down at the police station their suppositions were based the other way around.

"She sees that there's something wrong," said Crosby,

"when there's that sort of money standing to her credit."

"And what would she do then?"

"Tell other people about it?" hazarded Crosby. "Tell the bank anyway, pronto."

"Somebody," said Sloan profoundly, "didn't want her to do that. They killed her instead."

"It doesn't get them very far, does it?" objected Crosby. "George Wansdyke would find out soon enough when he began to wind her affairs up."

"Time," said Sloan. "They might only have been buying time." As a sounding board there was no doubt that Crosby lacked something. "Wansdyke's pretty busy, what with being in sole charge while his partner's away and a—what did they call it—a new product launching on hand."

"Talking of time," said Crosby helpfully, "it's always opening time for Dr. Peter McCavity. And, sir, we don't know how badly Nurse Petforth wants to get married, do we?"

"Or how much any of the others needed their share," conceded Sloan, adding, "if the money was really Beatrice Wansdyke's to leave." There was definitely something in the way of thought burgeoning at the back of his mind now. "There's always the possibility that she might have found what she was looking for." Air into money: it was a nice thought.

"If time came into it," said Crosby a little truculently, "it would be because something was going to happen, wouldn't it?" He smoothed the bedclothes in front of him. "Well, nothing's happened so far, sir, has it, and there's nothing due to happen either, is there?"

"Not that we know about," temporised Sloan. He cast his mind over the Wansdyke legatees. Nothing important appeared to be pending. "We don't know everything, of course."

"It's a bit hard," observed the detective constable, following a different tack, "if she's got to die just to stop her beetling round to her bank manager to tell him that somebody's turned over two pages or something. . . ."

"Doesn't make sense, does it?" agreed Sloan absently.

"I wonder where the quarter of a million pounds did come from?"

Sloan nodded. "Me, too."

"Someone must use that sort of money," said the constable. "Business, I suppose."

"If the money wasn't lost, stolen, or strayed," assented Sloan, "that's pretty well all that's left." The dog had died, too; he mustn't forget that.

"Big business," said Crosby comfortably. There was less than five pounds in the locker by his bed.

Detective Inspector Sloan stood up, ready to go back to the maternity ward. "Business. We'll have to look into . . ." His voice faded to a standstill. "Say that again, Crosby," he commanded, an entirely different tone in his voice.

"Business," said Crosby. "Big business."

"We were talking about something that might be due to happen, weren't we?" he said, suppressing a rising excitement.

"Nothing that we could think of," Crosby reminded him.

"Oh, yes, Crosby, there is something due to happen."

"Sir?"

"On Friday morning."

"Friday?" Crosby looked up. "Tomorrow?"

"As ever was." Sloan had a memory of not one but two occasions when a desperate public relations man had been chasing a managing director about a press release. "Beatrice Wansdyke didn't die because of a clerical error," he breathed with new-found conviction.

"No?" Crosby struggled to sit up in bed.

"No," he said softly. "It was all planned most beautifully, Crosby." Light was dawning fast. Someone had wanted burial, not cremation. Cremation called for two medical certificates, not one.

"What was?"

"Oh, yes," continued Sloan to himself, "in due course George Wansdyke would have indeed discovered the money and been able to prove that it wasn't Beatrice's. . . ."

"Would he?"

"But by then," said Sloan grimly, "it would have been too late."

"Too late for what?" insisted Crosby, pushing the bedclothes aside.

Sloan wasn't listening.

"Too late for what?" repeated Crosby.

Sloan's mind was racing ahead now with a speed that would have shamed a computer.

"I'm beginning to see it all now."

"I'm not, sir."

"Wansdyke and Darnley couldn't have their new product launching until Friday for a reason."

Crosby merely looked bewildered.

"Because of something that was going to happen to-day, Crosby."

"Nothing was due to happen today," protested the detective constable.

"Oh, yes there was."

"Thursday?"

"Today's Thursday," said Sloan authoritatively, "and something's due to happen. Something we'd forgotten about."

"We knew?"

"Everyone knew," said Sloan. "That was the beauty of it."

"What?"

"Something the murderer was waiting for." He shot a look at his watch and snapped, "Where's the nearest telephone? Quickly."

* * *

Several things happened at once.

Detective Constable Crosby flung back the bed-clothes. Detective Inspector Sloan raced across the ward. A ward maid called Nellie began a stately pro-gression down between the row of beds with a bucket and mop. Sloan side-stepped Nellie but Crosby can-noned into her. Sloan reached Sister Fleming's office and the telephone at much the same time as Sister

Fleming emerged to enquire into the noise and confusion.

Sloan pushed straight past her and grabbed the telephone directory. With savagely controlled speed he started hunting through its flimsy pages, muttering under his breath the while. "Darnley . . . where are the D's. . . . Don't anyone tell me that they're after the C's. . . ."

Nobody tried to do that.

"Mr. Crosby," an outraged sister was saying, "get back to bed at once."

"Darnley," said Sloan again, rapidly running his finger down a column. "Darnley . . . what's his first name? . . . I remember," he said before Crosby had time to speak ". . . it's Malcolm, isn't it? . . . George Wansdyke told us that . . . here we are."

Sister Fleming drew herself up to her full height.

Nobody took any notice.

"Darnley, M.C.P.," shouted Sloan, "Selborne . . . why can't people use street numbers instead of house names? . . . Acacia Avenue, Berebury." He was already dialling as he spoke. "Acacia Avenue isn't as good an address as the one the Wansdykes live at," he remarked as his fingers went round the dialling digits. He heard the bell ring at the other end and answered his own observation with "But then Malcolm Darnley didn't marry a Hartley-Powell."

"Mr. Crosby . . ." thundered Sister Fleming, "what are you doing out of bed?"

The telephone bell rang three times at the house called Selborne in Acacia Avenue before it was answered.

"Mrs. Darnley?" said Sloan with suppressed urgency.

"Speaking." She had a pleasant light voice.

"Do you happen to know which flight your husband is travelling back from the United States on?"

"Who is that?" she asked more sharply. "Do you know what the time is?"

"Police," jerked out Sloan. "Not about an accident or anything." If he believed in crossing fingers he would have crossed them now. "Just a few enquiries."

"At this hour?"

"His flight number," said Sloan martially. "Do you know that?"

"No."

"The time then," said Sloan quickly.

"I do know he's due to land at about seven o'clock this morning."

"Our time?" In his youth Sloan had read *Around the World in Eighty Days*. The last chapter had made a lasting impression on him.

"Our time," said Mrs. Darnley calmly. "Why do you want to know?"

"How is he planning to get home?"

"From the airport, you mean?"

"Yes. Are you meeting him, for instance?"

"Oh, no. He'll have landed by now, won't he?"

Sloan shot a quick look at his watch and groaned inwardly.

"He's coming home by car," she volunteered.

"Whose car?" Sloan fought to keep the rising anxiety out of his voice.

"His own. Ours, that is. I don't drive, you see." She coughed. "Malcolm thinks the fewer people who drive the better, especially wives."

"Where did he leave it?" Sloan heroically refrained from other comment.

"In the airport car park. We don't mind it being out in the open." She laughed. "It's so old that no one would steal it now."

Sloan interrupted her without ceremony. "What's the registration number?"

"Let me see . . . I should know, shouldn't I, after all these years."

Sloan waited. The seconds seemed like minutes.

"But I'm not very good at remembering numbers," she said apologetically. "Is it important?"

"Yes," said Sloan between clenched teeth, adding under his breath, "madam, you don't know how important."

"You'll be able to find it easily enough in a crowd," she said brightly, "if that's what you want."

"How?"

"It'll be the oldest one there."

"Mrs. Darnley . . ."

"Bound to be," she said confidently. "We don't believe in planned obsolescence, you see, so we never
change cars until we have to."

Sloan rigorously suppressed something about not be-
lieving in fairies himself and said instead with rigid for-
mality, "Thank you, madam. You've been a great
help."

"Are you sure, Officer, that there's nothing wrong?"
asked Mrs. Darnley.

But by then Sloan had rung off.

*   *   *

Malcolm Darnley, partner in Messrs. Wansdyke and
Darnley, did not look like an agitator. Therein, as all
experienced bureaucrats and administrators knew, lay
half his strength. His essentially mild manner and con-
ventional dress invariably strengthened his case at public enquiries.

At the moment the archconservationist looked just
what he was—a tired businessman. With jet-lag weari-
ness he walked across the airport car park, humping his
luggage with him. A wasteland, he thought to himself,
as he regarded row upon row of parked cars. Being a
methodical soul, he had made a mental note of exactly
where he'd left his own before leaving on his trip.

Not that he couldn't pick out his own vehicle easily
enough anyway. It was the oldest car in sight. And the
best maintained. He spotted it without delay and
walked towards it with affection. If every owner cherished their mechanical appliances in the way the Darn-
leys did there would be fewer municipal dumps. He
looked at more modern productions of the assembly
line with complacency. They didn't make cars like his
any more.

It was parked some little distance from the entrance
and he picked his way round the rows, wishing his luggage wasn't quite so heavy. He turned his head for a
moment when he heard a distant shout but then carried
on. He had almost reached the row where his own car

was waiting when the shout came again. It was nearer now.

Malcolm Darnley continued walking. After all, no one knew him here. He did just check over his belongings to make sure he hadn't dropped his wallet or anything. All seemed well and he strode onwards.

Next time the shout was clearly audible.

Darnley turned and saw a running policeman. It was, he conceded to himself, an unusual sight. Policemen didn't usually run: something important must be happening. A quick scanning of the horizon did not reveal to Malcolm Darnley what that could be. Shaking his head to himself, he forged on.

The shout came again.

This time there was no doubt as to whom it was addressed.

Himself.

The policeman was running in his direction and shouting at him at the same time.

Darnley had reached his own car now. He dumped his travelling bag down and turned, fumbling in his pocket for his keys. He would just park his luggage in the car. . . .

This time he heard what it was that the policeman was shouting. It was for him to keep still.

Essentially co-operative except in the matter of conservation of the countryside and the preservation of England's architectural heritage, Malcolm Darnley, thorn in much bureaucratic executive flesh, stood still.

As well as the running policeman, other figures were now appearing at the gallop from other corners of the airport car park.

Malcolm Darnley was quite bewildered. He looked around at the car park. It seemed normal enough to him. He cast an eye over his own car. That, too, looked just as he had left it. . . . He stiffened. . . . Well, no, not quite.

He, Malcolm Darnley, had not left a newspaper draped carelessly over the back seat before flying to the United States. Certainly not an Irish newspaper.

The running policeman skidded to a halt beside him

and put out his hand for Darnley's car keys. "If you don't mind, sir . . ."

Darnley surrendered them without demur.

He was no fool. This was no time for protest. Instead he stood back and waited for an explanation. It came from an unexpected quarter. One of the other figures who had converged on his car turned out to be an expert in his own particular rarefied field. Civilised life is under threat in more ways than by the simple despoliation of the countryside. Malcolm Darnley learned that today's airport carries its own bomb-disposal expert on the staff.

The specialist's first requirement was that everyone move well back before he commenced operations.

Obediently, Malcolm Darnley—no nonconformist in essentials—joined in the general retreat. They all watched the explosives man working at his lonely job from a safe distance.

It was not long before he reported back.

"If," he said to a bemused Malcolm Darnley, "you had touched your ignition switch you'd have been blown to kingdom come."

"Why?" asked Malcolm Darnley.

Chapter 18

Sometimes their goods are swallowed by the sea,
And sometimes they come safely back to port.

Police Superintendent Leeyes was never at his best first thing in the morning. Somewhere about the time when the lark took over from the nightingale his natural acerbity rose. And continued to rise.

This morning ws no exception.

"Will someone kindly tell me," he said with icy impatience, "exactly what has been going on?"

He was sitting squarely behind his desk glaring at Sloan.

Sloan immediately made to speak.

Leeyes forestalled him. "I come in to find a man— Nicholas Petforth no less—in the cells who you"—he flashed an aggressive look at the detective inspector— "keep telling me isn't guilty."

"Isn't guilty of murdering Beatrice Wansdyke," reiterated Sloan: not for the first time.

"And," carried on Leeyes imperviously, "to be given a message over the telephone."

"A message, sir?" Sloan started forward eagerly.

"I pick up that"—here he directed a malevolent stare in the direction of the telephone receiver on his desk which he had just replaced with altogether unnecessary vigor. Telephone cradles did not last long in his office.

"Yes?" Sloan was right on the edge of his chair now.

"To be told, Sloan, something that doesn't make sense."

"What?" asked Sloan urgently. It was all very well

183

for people to say that a man shouldn't get too involved with his work but . . .

"Why," Leeyes demanded grandly, "should I have a message for you, Sloan, from a bomb-disposal expert?"

Sloan began to speak. "Sir . . ."

"And tell me," carried on the superintendent, "why he should wish you to be told that there was a quantity of explosive packed under the bonnet of a car with the registration number of . . ." He glanced down at the message sheet.

"I know the car," said Sloan weakly.

"And that," said Leeyes, "there was enough of it to be sure of killing the driver."

Sloan relaxed. "We were in time then . . ."

"In time for what?"

"To save a life."

"Ah, yes." Superintendent Leeyes had all the irascible man's maddening imperturbability about the big things of this world. "He said something else too." The superintendent frowned at his own handwriting. "I know what it was."

"Sir?"

"That if the balloon had gone up . . ."

"Yes?"

"They would have been lucky to have found so much as his collar stud."

"Ah . . ." Sloan let out a sigh of pure relief.

"Sloan," he said with mock gentleness: menacingly.

"Sir?"

"Whose collar stud?"

"Malcolm Darnley's," said Sloan happily.

"Malcolm Darnley of Wansdyke and Darnley?"

Sloan nodded. "You see, sir, when I came to think of it, it was the only thing that hadn't happened yet."

"What was?"

"His coming home tomorrow . . . today, I mean." That reminded Sloan of something. "Sir, I must be getting back to the hospital as quickly as I can."

"What had his coming home got to do with Beatrice Wansdyke?" insisted Leeyes. You didn't get to be superintendent without being able to override the wishes of other people when it suited you.

"I'm not quite sure . . . yet . . . it was something Crosby said."

"Crosby?" echoed Leeyes in tones of pure disbelief.

"About the source of the money."

"Out of the mouths of babes," conceded Leeyes.

"If it wasn't inheritance or the proceeds of a tidy-sized job . . ." Babes. Sloan kept still with difficulty. He shouldn't be here at all really. Not now.

"We know it wasn't any of them," said Leeyes impatiently. "We checked on all those early on." That "early on" was Tuesday and today was Thursday surprised neither of them. Each criminal investigation had its own timetable: Sloan would not be surprised to know that someone was still looking for Jack the Ripper. There might even be a warrant out for Cain. . . .

"So," went on Sloan, "when Crosby said what about it being big business money . . ."

"I suppose," mused the superintendent, "when you think of some payroll snatches . . ."

"Big business wouldn't think that sort of money so very out of the way," pursued Sloan. "At least, I don't think it would." He had himself been schooled on the principle that murder most foul could be done for a hatpin let alone a hat but it didn't mean that there wasn't an opposite end to the same scale.

"So?" Orders of magnitude didn't interest the superintendent.

"The only business round here that had anything to do with the case is . . ."

"I know," growled Leeyes. "Don't tell me."

"Wansdyke and Darnley."

Leeyes grunted. "That well-known Berebury firm."

"Well known in the plastics field anyway," said Sloan. He'd been doing what research he could in the last half hour.

"I don't see the connection," objected Leeyes.

"Neither do I, sir, yet."

"And I thought"—Leeyes was adept at shifting responsibility whenever he could—"from what you said that George Wansdyke was about the only one who didn't stand to benefit from what his aunt left in her will."

"That was the beauty of the whole thing, sir," breathed Sloan, spoiling the effect by adding in a cautionary way, "I think."

Leeyes started to raise an objection.

"I'm hoping," interposed Sloan swiftly, "that a chat with Malcolm Darnley will put us in the picture."

"And in the meantime?"

Sloan told him exactly what he proposed doing in the meantime.

*　*　*

Margaret Sloan wasn't asleep any longer.

Far from it.

Sloan had begun to frame uncertain sentences as he hurried along the corridor to the maternity unit. They faded from his lips as he entered the delivery room.

"Margaret . . ."

She put out her hand.

"You got my message," he began as he stepped swiftly to her side.

He had sent Crosby down from Fleming Ward with it, reckoning that, next to a white coat, the wearing of pyjamas, dressing gown, and bandage gave one the easiest entrée to almost everywhere in the hospital. Almost everywhere. Not to this ward, of course. He'd have got as far as the door though. Even Crosby.

His wife looked at him almost without recognition, her mind elsewhere.

"A job," he said uneasily. "I was on a job."

Wordlessly she tightened her grip on his hand.

Someone masked and gowned told him where to stand. He looked up. The voice behind the mask was familiar. He'd heard it before.

"Inspector Sloan, I presume," said the man.

He nodded. It was like studying an Identikit picture without hair, nose, and chin: and as tantalising.

Margaret Sloan was trying to say something.

He immediately turned back to her.

At first no sound came.

He put his head near her lips.

"Never off duty," she whispered, "are you?"

"My dearest love . . ."

He started to perspire.

Those lonely souls who had never travelled far in love missed this road too.

The midwife was saying something behind her mask now.

Sloan moistened his lips. A man tended to forget that the Ship of Felicity once embarked upon berthed here. He wondered if a woman ever did.

"Coming up to crowning, doctor," said the midwife more clearly.

So this was what they meant by that.

Love's majesty wore a crown and this was it.

He found himself taking deep gulps of breath, matching Margaret's. The French had a word for the pain that husbands suffered. . . . Someone had once told him what it was. *Couvade*. It had had no meaning at the time. . . .

There was a moment not long after that when it crossed Sloan's mind that being born from Adam's rib in a deep sleep must be a better way than this.

Once he remembered looking at his watch but it meant nothing now: time didn't enter this world.

It was Thursday, that was all.

Thursday's child has far to go.

A sudden scurrying among the professionals told him this child—Thursday's child—his child—was making a move.

It was just a little later when, though he didn't quite realise it in so many words, Sloan became deeply committed to the Classical Greek School Midwifery. Had anyone asked him then and there he would have opted for his child springing—like Athena—fully armed from the forehead of Zeus.

Presently that feeling, too, passed when they all— man, woman, and child—became submerged in a welter of clinical activity and ordinary human excitement.

Then the man in the mask spoke again. He recognised the voice now. It belonged to Dr. Roger Elspin. He said, "Inspector Sloan, you have a son."

* * *

It didn't seem wholly right that the first person to congratulate him should be a furtive little man lurking outside in the maternity ward corridor.

"What are you doing here, Larky?" asked Sloan from all the eminence of cloud nine.

"Same as you, Inspector. Being a father."

"I'll tell the midwife to keep an eye on her watch."

"Not on my account. I'm going straight these days," insisted Larky Nolson earnestly. "Honest."

"Honest? You wouldn't know the meaning of the word, Larky. . . ." Sloan floated on.

And the second person: a detective constable with a bandage around his head. But fully dressed now. Sloan seized on him.

"Come on, Crosby. We know where to go now."

"Do we, sir? Which way?"

"Wansdyke and Darnley's, of course. Where else did you think?"

* * *

There was a little portable radio on George Wansdyke's desk in his office. It was tuned in to the programme that broadcasts snippets of news as they come in and the latest news every hour on the hour. In between news flashes and weather reports a disc jockey plays pop record after pop record. There was, however, no one in the office listening to it.

"He was here a minute ago," insisted a mystified secretary. "If you'll just wait I'll check to see if he's gone through to the works."

"Thank you," said Sloan, moving over to Wansdyke's desk. There was just one memo on it. It was handwritten and was addressed to Bill Benfleet, Public Relations Manager, and was from George Wansdyke, Joint Managing Director. It was marked URGENT and it read:

Subject: Tomorrow's new product announcement. This is to be cancelled forthwith and all press releases and publicity material recalled at once.

Detective Inspector Sloan motioned Crosby to collect the memo. "We'll need that," he said.

"Exhibit A," commented Crosby. "It's the only one we've got."

"There's an empty insulin bottle," Sloan reminded him, "and some explosive clamped to a car. . . ."

"And a dead dog," added Crosby lugubriously. "I'd forgotten Isolde."

"A funny mixture, I grant you." Sloan frowned. "I reckon this memo was meant to be sent as soon as Wansdyke heard news of the explosion and his partner's death on the radio."

"And it didn't come." Crosby grinned. "Did it?"

"We can't find Mr. Wansdyke," said the secretary, coming back into the room. "I've tried Research and Development—he's often there—and the lab and the moulding shop. . . ."

A telephone rang. She picked it up. "When. . . . when? Oh, I see. Thank you . . . I'll tell him." She put down the receiver. "That was the man on the gate. He says Mr. Wansdyke left just after you arrived, Inspector, by car."

"Which way did he go?" interrupted Crosby.

"He says he took the Kinnisport Road. . . ."

"The hoverport," said Sloan quickly.

"He won't get far."

* * *

The subsequent road chase made traffic history in the county of Calleshire.

"I take it," said Superintendent Leeyes coldly later that morning, "that you are prepared to appease Inspector Harpe. I shall reprimand Constable Crosby myself."

"We got our man," said Sloan simply. It was the police exegesis.

Crosby's turn of speed at the wheel had indicated complete recovery from his head injuries. George Wansdyke's could only point to total guilt. The latter was, however, not saying anything to anyone.

"Which means," declared Leeyes heavily, "that you'll have to do the explaining, Sloan."

"It's easier now that I've had a word with Malcolm Darnley," admitted Sloan. "It was guesswork until then."

Leeyes waited.

"It all happened the way it did," began Sloan slowly, "because Malcolm Darnley had a business trip to the States scheduled."

"Go on."

"That meant that George Wansdyke couldn't kill him when he wanted to."

"Hard luck," said Leeyes vigorously.

"He just wasn't there to be killed," said Sloan. "It all hung on that."

"You couldn't be oversimplifying things, could you?" enquired the superintendent sarcastically. "Why should Darnley come home and be killed?"

"Not long before he went off on this trip," said Sloan, "the firm of Wansdyke and Darnley came up with a discovery. . . ."

"Not Miss Wansdyke's do-it-yourself kit for making money out of air?"

"No. A discovery about plastic—an important one."

"Ah, now we're getting somewhere."

"That's what Malcolm Darnley and George Wansdyke thought—each in his own way." Sloan paused. "The trouble was that their ways were different ones."

"It happens with partners," said Leeyes sagely. "They don't always see eye to eye."

Sloan cleared his throat. "That was a bit of an understatement in this case."

"Especially marriage partners."

"The discovery," said Sloan hastily, "according to Malcolm Darnley was both socially important and highly marketable."

"Bound to be troublesome then," said Leeyes cynically.

"Not so much a discovery," Sloan forged on, "as a new process involving a . . . a"—he shot a quick glance down at his notebook—"a synergist."

Superintendent Leeyes did not speak. He just looked.

"It's like a catalyst but different," faltered Sloan. It was no use. You couldn't bone up someone else's trade over the telephone in a few minutes, especially when that person had just escaped death by a whisker and naturally wanted to know why. "A catalyst," he continued in an unusually hortatory manner, "causes a reaction but remains unchanged by it."

"And a synergist?" enquired Leeyes silkily.

"Causes a reaction but is itself changed in the process. It—er—potentiates things."

"Like murder?"

"This . . . ingredient"—that was an easier word altogether. He would use it from now on. "The ingredient," he continued, "used in this new process they'd stumbled on will make some sorts of plastic eventually decay."

"Is that good or bad?" As far as the superintendent was concerned it was a black and white world.

"Used plastic is a great problem to society," said Sloan, parrotlike. Listening to Malcolm Darnley was infectious. "Your old yoghourt carton stands to last longer than the Sphinx. . . ."

"Well?"

"With this ingredient built in it would gradually become . . . er"—he hesitated before introducing yet another new word—"degradable and so decay."

Leeyes, however, wasn't thinking about words. "This process, Sloan, was worth money?"

"Big money," agreed Sloan tacitly.

"A quarter of a million pounds' worth of money?"

"Precisely, sir." He coughed. "Exactly, you might say."

"What then," asked Leeyes simply, "was the problem?"

Detective Inspector Sloan felt a momentary pang of sympathy for George Wansdyke as he tried to explain. "Malcolm Darnley was a conservation buff, sir. Mad about preserving the countryside."

"We all know that," said Leeyes. "What about it?"

"Malcolm Darnley," said Sloan impressively, "thought that the world should have the process free."

"Pro bono publico," breathed Leeyes, awe-struck, "instead of a quarter of a million pounds?"

"No more plastic cups in the Channel," said Sloan, echoing a fanatic. "No more cows choking to death on plastic bags left in a field. Less detritus for eternity."

The superintendent was considering something quite different—something more in his own line. "There are more ways than one of killing the golden goose," he said. Smaller rubbish dumps didn't excite him. Murder did.

"That's what Wansdyke thought," reported Sloan. The greatest good of the greatest number hadn't suited George Wansdyke at all. "He lost out in the argument with Darnley but he did manage to get him to agree to defer a public announcement until Darnley got back from the States."

"His death warrant."

"Everything was to stay under wraps until then."

Leeyes grunted. "Breathing space."

"He managed that side of things quite well."

"Businesses," said Leeyes largely, "are used to trade secrets."

"Wansdyke apparently made quite a thing of insisting that Malcolm Darnley himself should be the one to do the announcing because of his connections with the conservation lobby."

"Conservation lobby!" Leeyes ground his teeth. "The man won't even let us cut off a branch let alone a tree."

"Wansdyke made out that Darnley would make the better splash in the press and so forth." Sloan was on sure ground here. Twice he'd seen Bill Benfleet, the firm's public relations man, closeted with a strangely reluctant Wansdyke, trying to get him to pass a press release for publication. "No wonder Wansdyke hadn't wanted to say too much."

"Knowing all the time," said the superintendent intelligently, "that there wasn't going to be any disclosing of trade secrets by anybody."

"Not if George Wansdyke could help it," said Sloan, "because he'd gone and sold the process to a big manufacturer while Darnley was away."

Leeyes whistled. "He had, had he?"

"He was in sole charge while Darnley was abroad," said Sloan. "There was no problem."

"Don't tell me," said Leeyes acidly, "that he didn't know what to do with the money."

"In a way," replied Sloan. *Embarras de richesses* was quite often a problem in the criminal world.

"If Darnley was abroad why couldn't Wansdyke have just paid it into the firm's account—he couldn't very well pretend it wasn't the firm's secret, could he?"

"No, it was the firm's secret all right. The people who bought it would have checked on that. Wansdyke couldn't pay it into the firm's account straightaway because Darnley got weekly sales figures while he was abroad and, anyway, anyone in the firm might have mentioned it to him in a letter. . . ." That he also got a cash-flow chart Sloan did not mention. He was a policeman not an accountant.

"What was wrong with using his own account in the meantime then?"

"He shares it with his wife."

Leeyes rolled his eyes at man's monumental folly.

"He could have opened a special account," said Sloan, who had been thinking about this, "but that has the definite look of misappropriation. He needed this transaction to seem quite above board."

"Clean hands."

"Exactly."

"With Darnley dead though," Leeyes reminded him.

"And Beatrice too," said Sloan. "She knew about the discovery, you see. She spent her weekends in the lab by courtesy of Darnley and she knew enough chemistry to understand what he'd discovered. He'd told her about their success."

"So with Darnley and Beatrice both dead . . ."

"And the money back in the firm's account as soon as possible after that," said Sloan.

"Everything neat and tidy for the auditors—that's always important in fraud." The superintendent leant back. "Do you know, Sloan, that you can nearly always put people who commit fraud into open prisons? Funny that they should be that sort of trustworthy, isn't it?"

Sloan kept a grip on his theme. "Wansdyke had already begun to write the firm he'd sold it to enquiring why he hadn't had their cheque."

"Window dressing," said Leeyes succinctly.

"They would say that they'd sent it to the bank as instructed, and the bank would say they'd been given the right name and account number for Miss B. G. Wansdyke."

"And?"

"George Wansdyke would say right name—B. G. Wansdyke—he's Bertram George himself, remember—but wrong account number. The money belongs to Wansdyke and Darnley and he can prove quite easily that it does. It was safe enough, of course, in Beatrice's account while he was sole executor."

"Everyone," said Leeyes drily, "says 'Oops, sorry' and blames the typist. And everything in the garden's lovely again."

"Beatrice had to die too because of what she knew. He was just taking advantage of the fact." Sloan coughed. "We haven't heard George Wansdyke's side of things yet, sir."

"He's not only not speaking to the police"—Leeyes poked at a message sheet on his desk—"he won't see his wife either."

Sloan clapped his hand to his forehead. "Wife! Good Lord, where's the nearest florist?"

"Ah yes," said Superintendent Leeyes pompously, "I hear that Wansdyke and Darnley aren't the only ones with a new product announcement, are they?"

"No, sir."

*　*　*

Detective Inspector Sloan had someone else to appease besides Inspector Harpe of Traffic Division.

He said it with flowers at the bedside each day.

Margaret Sloan had a lot of visitors. "They're going to get married after Briony's taken her final state," she informed him one day.

"Who is . . . are?"

"Dr. Elspin and Briony Petforth." She smiled dreamily. "He's really very nice."

"For a doctor," Sloan reminded her.

"That will give them a little time to save up." Margaret Sloan paused. "She still gets her aunt's house, doesn't she?"

"Oh, yes," said Sloan drily. "Everything except the quarter of a million pounds goes just where Miss Wansdyke willed it. She only lost out on one thing she wanted."

"What was that?"

"Her wish to be cremated." Sloan shifted uncomfortably. Visitors' chairs in hospitals were not designed for long use. "Cremation means two doctors and a lot more questions all round. Wansdyke didn't want that. He wanted a nice quick death certificate."

"He did it, then? Changed the insulin for water?"

"Oh, yes," said Sloan. "As nice a way to murder as you can find."

"Nice?" She shuddered.

"Nice legally," he said. That means the police didn't like it but the lawyers did. "The superintendent thinks they'll have to go for malice aforethought in a big way."

Margaret Sloan smoothed the edge of the sheet. "And the dog?"

"He killed that, too. He had a key, remember. He didn't want an Airedale barking when Beatrice drifted off into her coma and it couldn't get out. Or if anyone called. Wansdyke had invited Briony to his house on Sunday, by the way."

"To make sure she didn't call on her aunt?"

"That's right. They could have saved her, you know, almost up until the end."

Margaret Sloan shuddered again.

Detective Inspector Sloan recalled himself away from one sort of duty and back to another. "How's my son and heir?"

*   *   *

On his next visit she asked him about Mrs. Pauline Wansdyke.

"Gone back to mother."

"Poor woman."

"She always thought she'd married beneath her," said Sloan, who had had to endure quite a lot of Mrs. Pauline Wansdyke lately.

"It never does to think that," said Margaret Sloan sagaciously.

"All the other Hartley-Powells said so too."

"That only makes it worse."

"They've traced the explosive that was under the car," he said soberly.

She shivered. "To George Wansdyke?"

"Without a shadow of doubt."

* * *

Another day she had news of Nicholas Petforth for him gleaned from his sister, Briony.

"He's very sorry about it all," Margaret Sloan began.

Sloan grunted. He hadn't a lot of time for young men who hit policemen, and said so now with some vigor. "And without a reason," he added pointedly.

"When he heard the police were asking after him"—Margaret Sloan repeated what an anxious Briony had told her—"he lost his nerve and left the squat and his job."

"Actions speak louder than words," observed Sloan.

"And of course as soon as George Wansdyke knew that somebody was suspicious about something he stirred things up as much as he could in that quarter."

"He certainly got Briony worried," conceded Sloan.

"And Nicholas through her," said his wife. She paused and adjusted a flower in the vase on her locker. "He realises now," said Margaret Sloan, surrogate apologetic from Briony Petforth, "that he was only running away."

"Why?"

She embarked on a delicate secondhand explanation. "There were—er—things going on at the squat that he—er—knew about."

"But didn't want to be asked about."

"They were his friends." She sketched a gesture in the air. "They have their loyalties in those places too."

"Luston Division raided it last night," said Sloan complacently.

"Briony will be pleased," beamed Mrs. Sloan. "That means Nicholas is in the clear, doesn't it? He wasn't really part of . . ." She stopped.

"What was going on?" Sloan finished for her kindly.

"Malcolm Darnley's taking him into the firm."

"There's more than one sort of sentence in this world," he said, amused.

"He says if they send Nicholas to prison he can use his time learning about plastics."

"Condemned to conformity at last." Sloan grinned. "Prison for assaulting a police officer in the execution of his duty would rate more highly at the Luston squat than a job as an executive."

"Malcolm Darnley says," she repeated with a matching twinkle in her eye, "that with so much extra capital in the firm they can afford a few mistakes by a new boy."

"Crosby's head's healing nicely," he said not entirely inconsequentially. "He'll make the christening without a bandage."

* * *

To no one's surprise Inspector Harpe was not as sanguine as everyone else.

"Dr. Peter McCavity's inheritance," he announced in his usual melancholy way, "is going to go the same way as his income."

"Down his throat?" supplied Sloan obligingly. "The way of all flesh was to the kitchen."

"And paying for the damage."

"It will have been George Wansdyke who rang in and reported that McCavity hit that bollard in Ridley Road," said Sloan. Even the outer pieces of the jigsaw puzzle were fitting in now. "On the Friday afternoon."

"Bit of an opportunist your chap, wasn't he?" said Harpe.

"Murderers usually are," said Sloan. "He must have
seen McCavity's car around when he was at the house
killing the dog."

"There's never any knowing what a drunken doctor
will get up to," said Happy Harry censoriously. The
traffic man had always been convinced that alcohol was
the devil in solution. "If Wansdyke was looking round
for someone to take the blame if there was trouble . . ."

"No wonder old Dr. Paston had his worries," mused
Sloan. "Got a lot on his mind, I daresay."

"McCavity went the wrong way round the station
roundabout last night," said Harpe, who was nothing if
not single-minded. "Mark my words, Sloan, that young
man's next traffic violation will be his last as a licenced
driver."

* * *

"Sloan." Superintendent Leeyes pushed the case papers back across the desk.

"Sir."

"I don't like loose ends."

"No, sir."

"Untidy."

"Yes, sir."

"There's something we haven't done."

"Is there, sir?" Sloan allowed himself the luxury of a
yawn. He felt as if he hadn't stopped doing things for
days and nights. "What's that?"

"Put the coroner right."

Sloan stiffened.

"You might just step round," said Leeyes civilly,
"and tell him we were right and he was wrong. With my
compliments, of course."

ABOUT THE AUTHOR

CATHERINE AIRD had never tried her hand at writing suspense stories before publishing *The Religious Body*—a novel which immediately established her as one of the genre's most talented writers. *A Late Phoenix, The Stately Home Murder, His Burial Too, Some Die Eloquent, Henrietta Who?* and *A Most Contagious Game* have subsequently enhanced her reputation. Her ancestry is Scottish, but she now lives in a village in East Kent, near Canterbury, where she serves as an aid to her father, a doctor, and takes an interest in local affairs.

WHODUNIT?

Bantam did! By bringing you these masterful tales of murder, suspense and mystery!